Fish Head Fever: A Story of Zombies, Mermaids and One Immortal Chihuahua

The Comstock Tails, Volume 1

Barbara Zoey Zimmerly

Published by Otis Publications, 2021.

FISH HEAD FEVER: A STORY OF ZOMBIES, MERMAIDS AND ONE IMMORTAL CHIHUAHUA

First edition. July 19, 2021.

Copyright © 2021 Barbara Zoey Zimmerly.

ISBN: 979-8201631314

Written by Barbara Zoey Zimmerly.

Chapter One

Joe Comstock, former tenth grader, sat on the port edge of his sloop, contemplating a brown glass bottle. "You're it," he said. "The last, the very last one." Joe drained the beer and threw the bottle in a slow wide arc. "Go. Become sea glass like your brothers before you."

Bored, he fingered the buckle on his life vest. His dad's, actually. He wished it had pockets.

The evening was clear. The sun, dropping through a thin bank of clouds on the horizon, gave a last, brilliant, eye-burning flash and sank out of sight.

The day had been okay. He'd exerted himself to sail under the Golden Gate Bridge and make a broad turn-around in the Bay before sailing south. Joe didn't recall any "red in the morning", but the barometer was on the low side...but not the first time, he thought. The air was cooling and he—tired of thinking about the past—double-checked his grocery list for tomorrow's port of call at Santa Cruz, went to his closet of a berth and called it a day.

#

"OW!"

Somehow Joe landed hard on his knees and then his shoulder. He wrapped his arms around his head as he tumbled in the dark. Half his body was wet! He pulled the cord on his life vest to inflate it, and stumbled toward the hatch. Joe reached for the latch pull but was thrown backwards onto the bunk.

Joe reviewed his options: *Stay here, drown. Go topside, probably drown.*

He staggered to standing and pushed on the hatch, again. No go. The screaming wind kept it shut. Joe gave all his weight to the hatch—nothing! The wind shifted on his third try and he lurched through to the wheelhouse. He hit the light switch and stared. Black walls rose around him—the boat dropping in a trough as the wave lifted to an impossible height, lethal and violent.

It paused for an instant, boasting its malevolence, and began to curl like a fist into a mythic surfer's pipeline: a massive, churning, collapse of water.

Joe's penultimate thought: *56 degrees Fahrenheit.*

Joe's last thought: *My turn.*

Chapter two

"He'll survive?"

Joe stirred at the man's gravelly voice.

"Certainly. Poor boy."

That was a delicate female voice.

"Certainly stupid."

His head hurt, but he was flat and warm and a powerful engine competently carried whatever vessel he was on. Sleep crooked its finger again, but the lovely female voice said, "Time to check out our young man. Can you open your eyes?"

He tried, but they were as good as stapled. Traitors! He wanted to see The Voice.

"Gilbert, would you get the lights, please? Young sailor, we can start with your name."

"Joe," he said, setting off painful wracking coughs that made his head hurt worse.

"Clear the pipes, boy," said Grumpy. Joe responded by throwing up. Magically, not on himself.

"Hmm. I would very much like to rule out concussion on our guest." Gentle hands were feeling his head. "Minimal lumps and bumps." The hands held his. "Squeeze my hands as hard as you can—Ooh! And now push your toes against my hands." The instant he could open his eyes she ruined the moment by shining a flashlight back and forth over his eyes.

"Report, Mellie?"

"No neurological deficits; air flow to the lungs is fine. Just a hard day at the office. Do you think, young Joe, that any of your bones are broken? Can you wiggle your toes? Tell me the date and where you are?"

Joe managed to blink at the very beautiful physician. Why does my doc looks like Sponge Bob, he thought. "Wanna get a burger?" He sounded like a bullfrog.

Grumpy laughed, "The boy is hitting on you."

"Let's try this again, Romeo. Can you tell me the date and where you are?"

Joe tried to think. "Uh, Friday, January the twenty-first, and near California?" Then, he stared. She really was beautiful.

"Excellent." She brought a can of soda and straw to his lips. "Stomach better, hmm?"

Joe pulled into his mouth the best ginger ale of his whole life and continued staring at the woman. He finally guessed she was letting him; she must be used to being stared at. Suddenly, his prefrontal cortex came to life.

"Where's my boat?"

Doc Beautiful looked over at Grumpy who said, "We're towing her."

"Hrhmm," Joe mumbled around the straw as two Tylenol entered his mouth. Swallowing obediently, he sank his pounding, globe-sized head on the soft thick pillow.

"Do you remember how you got here?"

"No." It was more a moan than a word.

Doc Beautiful said, "We'll leave you to rest." Joe opened one eye hoping to see more of her—better that than the violence of the wave that was returning to his mind. Joe got a side view and watched her carefully extracting the straw from his soda can before she closed the door.

He awoke to see the last of the sun dip into quiet waters off starboard. He'd lost a whole day! They were headed south. Hurting absolutely everywhere, Joe hoisted himself out of sickbay, up a ladder topside and into early twilight...and, as his eyes cleared the deck, stared into a massive tail filling his vision. A fish tail, a seven-foot-long fish tail with deep end-fins a yard wide and perfect scales in a khaki-green camo pattern, was lying on the deck.

Who caught that?

One more cautious step, and Joe saw that it was attached to a man in a deck chair sporting a flak jacket. Joe felt kind of sick. "Uhh. I'm going back to bed."

"Join us," said the man.

Grumpy? Grumpy's a fish?!

Another extremely anxious step—and Joe was looking at a deep ivory tail, covered with what looked like old scrimshaw carving, blended into a second man wearing a blue military shirt.

"Pull up a chair," said Scrimshaw.

Joe shook his head. "I'm hallucinating...I'm *hallucinating!*"

"It's okay, son," continued Scrimshaw, ignoring his hysterics. "Allegedly you were on a boat. What's her name?"

"The *Sea Wren*".

"Out of ..."

"Seattle." Joe watched Scrimshaw enter what he had said onto his ipad. *I bet he's the captain and Grumpy is some psycho freeloader.*

"And you're not Dominic Comstock, correct? He's your dad?"

Joe nodded.

"Hmm", said the maybe captain. "Dominic Comstock has quite the security clearance, Gilbert. And two months ago he was reported lost at sea." He stopped. He looked up to study the teen's face before him. "What in blazes were you doing sailing down the coast in February, *alone*?"

"That's my business! You're towing my boat, right?" he looked at Grumpy called Gilbert. "Where is it?"

"Where is it?" Gil shook his head. "At the bottom of the sea, bucko."

"You said...you said!" Joe let his fury out in words.

"Swears like a sailor, Gil," said Scrimshaw, mildly impressed. No words from Gil, but a deep rumbling began. It emanated from his belly and rolled down his powerful camo tail and somehow through Joe's own body! It put his muscles on edge, like a warning...

And then he was flying towards the water!

Joe sputtered and flailed and splashed, not the best swimmer as his solid chest made him stone-like. As he kicked unhappily to the outside ladder, a dolphin came alongside him to ease him along...except it wasn't a dolphin. It was a mermaid. A girl mermaid. A grown-up girl mermaid!

"Up, up you go."

But Joe held gripped the ladder and twisted to stare. "I'm hallucinating?"

"Go!" He climbed; she followed.

Out of the wind, wrapped in a blanket and staring at three fish tails—the mermaid's was a shiny bronze and gold—in reclining deck chairs, Joe slowly began to believe he was not hallucinating.

"Please to tell me why you put our guest in the water," the modest mermaid with a bikini top asked the one called Gil, formerly known as Grumpy. She selected a tiny fish from a bucket and popped it in her mouth and passed it to Scrimshaw.

An excellent question, thought Joe.

"Merely testing his flotation ability."

As he watched, the lovely woman with the most beautiful coppery skin he'd ever seen shook the water from her hair. It was instantly dry! *Mermaids have water-proof hair?*

"You're mermaids, huh?"

"Mermaids don't exist, dolt."

"We call ourselves 'swimmers,'" she said, smiling at him. "You may call me Luz." Then she tilted her head in mild reproof toward the unpredictable Gil creature whose tail muscles continued to ripple like an anaconda beneath its camo scales. It had an unsettling likeness to a cat's twitching tail.

Luz checked her phone and said, "You may wish to know, Gilberto, that he is times three."

"What?!" Gil looked incredulous. "Retest him. He can't even swim."

"I'm times three? Retest...what!" In his mind, Joe saw the straw from the ginger ale in Doc Beautiful's hand. "She tested my DNA from the straw!"

"Fuzznuts has some gray cells," said Gil.

Angry and so confused he couldn't sit, Joe stood with fists doubled, wanting to punch anything that moved. Gil popped a tiny fish from the bucket into his mouth. "Chill out, boy. Let the lovely Luz run the test again." He passed the bait bucket to Luz Marina who nibbled daintily on another herring.

"No way! I don't have to chill out. I don't have to do anything!" All three ignored him. As Joe watched, their end fins began to shrink and the skin wrinkled as toes began to form. He felt wobbly. "I need something to eat. I think I'm getting low blood sugar like my Grandma."

"A moment, *por favor*?" asked the lovely woman, whose feet had reappeared with impressively thick ankles.

Gil tossed her a towel and wrapped one around his waist. "Turn around, dolt. She's getting dressed."

I'm blushing? Okay...not a hallucination. Instead, Joe stared as Grumpy Gil's tail somehow reabsorbed into his legs.

"Later, Captain. Luz? I'll meet you at the lab." Gil walked away.

"Word to the wise?" The captain looked at Joe. "He's no fan of stupid."

#

"And now...the test. A pinprick, *por favor*." A droplet of blood on his fingertip was sucked up a channel onto a test strip just like his Grandma's blood sugar meter. But this read: HLA-B*84 expressionX3. "Is the same, times three. *Definitivamente* positive, but that is not a thorough breakdown of the DNA. We can make that later, if you wish."

"Times three *what*?" Joe said. He might as well have asked how purple smelled. Now Doc Beautiful and Gil came into the cramped laboratory space. Luz Marina told them the results.

"Times three, Mellie!" said Gil. "The boy should have gills."

The brunette beauty eased herself next to Joe. "Perhaps it is time I introduce myself. I am Melusine Vidmorya, a biochemist, ethno-geneticist, oceanographer...and physician."

Melusine held out her hand and he took it. The excessively educated woman held it gently, compassionately. That made Joe afraid, more afraid than in the storm. "I suggest that you sit while Luz Marina and I compare some figures. Have you eaten yet? And how did you get wet...?" She followed Joe's accusing glance. "Gil? Honestly! Let him change. We'll eat topside in fifteen."

#

Topside, the ladies were having fish tacos while Gil handed Joe—now in his own set of USCG sweats—a mound of chipped something in sauce in a bun. One bite had him moaning, "Dude! So good!"

"Mess specialty...creamed foreskins."

Joe barely paused, but pushed in a big mouthful as a ghost of a smile brightened Gil's tanned sea face. Jerk, thought Joe. Gil sat down and, again, spread his camo tail next to Luz Marina's metallic one.

Melusine continued, "Now, as concerns you, young sailor Joe, I am the director of the Genetics Institute for the Protection and Advancement of Sea Creatures. GI-PASC. Especially the protection and advancement of sea HUMANS." She paused solicitously as he rinsed down the last of the roll, and let her legs transform into the third glorious tail of the company, this one a rich tropical turquoise that matched her eyes.

"Of which you are one."

Chapter three

"No I'm not!" Joe jumped up. "I can't do *that*," he shouted at her tail. "If I were a, a *sea* human, I could make a tail. Dudes, I can hardly swim. I'm allergic to shrimp, and, and...times three? Please Doc, last time—times three *what*?!"

Gil and Luz Marina sat quietly, looking at Melusine. "Allow me to begin at the beginning. First, all that we know of our past comes from the genetic record of DNA. Soft tissue leaves no fossil record, nor does the sea." A few deft motions and she handed Joe her iPad. An outlined world map covered the screen with occasional concentrations of dots on the coastlines.

"The first sea people came on land about one million years after early man, Homo habilis, left Africa." She moved an elegant finger over the screen. "See the dots? Those are the places where we came ashore: Australia, India, Siberia, South Africa, Central America and northern Europe. We share genetic information with extinct land humans called Denisovans. And when archeo-geneticists test our blood, they credit only the Denisovans, as we don't exist." Melusine smiled at Joe's reaction. "Yes, it is difficult to understand. To simplify, sea humans came out of the oceans and began mating with land humans. The genetic item we identify as sea human is the HLA-B*84 which has its own little quirks. For example..." Somehow, Melusine added a bright red stripe to her tail that oscillated like a barber's pole. "Is that enough information to start with?"

Stone-face Gil said, "You're showing off. And you—" pointing to Joe—"Sit."

"And the three times HLA...?" persisted the new, resistant, sea human now seated.

"Profesora, why don't you answer this?" said Melusine. "Our Luz Marina is a specialist in Sea Human genetics."

"*Qué rica!*" Luz Marina licked bits of fish taco off her fingers. "Think of it in this way, Joe. You have from your parents three helpings—helpings? I'm still hungry—of B84 out of a possible four helpings, no? Two from one parent, one from the other. Most people have no helpings. And most everyone on this boat has only two. Two is enough to make the tail to come and to go. Three makes the gills and makes you to breathe underwater. And most of the ocean peoples have all the four. You see?"

"Not really."

Melusine picked up. "She gave you the simple explanation. There are all those 137 quirks too, making the full picture very complex. And the extraordinary thing is that with all the Sea Human DNA you are carrying, you exhibit no active traits. As Gil said, you can't even swim."

"I have a muscular chest," Joe defended himself. "I don't float."

Melusine smiled, as if to a little boy. "You seem to be as we are. The *true* sea humans—who have four B84—are what we were *before* coming on land. They look different, but the main difference is that they cannot transform their tails to legs and back. And they have permanent gills."

Gil lifted his beer, his motion philosophical. "God made the True, man made the Merm."

Joe realized his hands were feeling his neck and dropped them. "And me? No gills on this boy."

"They're below your pits," said Gil. Joe dropped his hands.

Dr. Melusine Vidmorya shrugged. "Have you heard of the science of epi-genetics?"

Joe shook his head.

"Each genetic trait has an on-switch. One can either be born with a trait which is switched on, or a mutation—perhaps from the action of a virus—can turn it on. The scientific community has been studying identical twins, asking questions like: Why does only one get a certain disease? Why does the switch go on in one and not the other? That is a large current area of study. For whatever reason, you did not switch on."

"It's too late, right? I can't like be a merm...whatever."

"It is doubtful that you would become a sea human. We know the switch, but not what activates it."

"I'll take 'doubtful'. Doubtful's good."

"However," continued Melusine, her face showing ongoing mental analysis as she spoke, "our data is scant and merely anecdotal."

Joe eyed her. "Has anyone else done this? Switch on?"

"In this generation, one. That is our scant data. Prior examples are from family histories."

"Okay, Doc, I'm good with that." Joe looked longingly at Gil and his bottle. "Ah, is there any more beer, sir?"

Gil tilted his bottle and drained it in the soft rosy hue of sunset. "All gone, Fuzznuts. We dock tomorrow in Monterey."

"Like where, exactly?" *Dude,* he thought, *I need a Visa card. I gotta call Dad's lawyer and get out of here.*

Sighing at his massive expenditure of tolerance, Gil explained, "We fished you out at Santa Cruz—top of the Bay. We dock at the bottom, at Monterey. By the way, the Captain and I would like to talk about your little jaunt down the coast. "

"It's a free ocean." He felt the smallest, threatening vibration coming towards him. Joe stiffened.

"Profesora," asked Melusine, "did you write the Director about the other genetic read-out similar to young Joe?" Luz Marina nodded, her cloud of curly hair swaying. The fading sunlight glowed on the circle of scaled flesh—turquoise, golden bronze and camo. Joe wished he could have had a beer...but sat very contently with his own hairy legs.

Having slept the sleep of the dead, Joe lie in his bunk. He missed his sloop, the buoyancy of it had swayed him like a cradle on the water. This bucket was huge in comparison, 154-feet long. A fast Sentinel Class Cutter made for quick response, said one of the sailors. All it did was vibrate. He rubbed his face, pushed his fingers through his hair and made his way to the galley, wearing the sweats he'd slept in. Joe was filling a bowl with scrambled eggs and two toasted bagels when Gil came in. *Too early for this dude.* "Are you like going to like dump me in the water again?"

Gil's weathered face had the emotion readability of a door. "That, Fuzznuts, like depends on you like saying like every sentence you like make."

"Like fair enough," said Joe, sitting at a skinny table and tucking into the heap of food. He loved that "like" irritated people, aka teachers, parents, and psychologists. "And the name's Joe."

Gil sipped some burnt-smelling coffee. "What are you good at, since there's no hope of you being a 'Swimmer'." He punctuated the word with finger quotes.

Joe knew this routine. He knew this question and its buddy, "What do you want to do with your life." The correct answers would produce the magic *ta-daa,* the perfect job choice. Next, you just had to work backwards, pick the perfect school with the right program and get in—provided you'd put in fourteen-hour days since grade school. He doubted he could out-antagonize Psycho Gil, so he answered the question based on his recent life. "Wrestling. Pool."

"Geometry?"

"Piece of cake." If this was The Talk, Gil was less irritating than Ma the Relentless: *"Study, your grades counts*—she'd started that one in fifth grade—*Learn a second language, like French, the French your mother 'as spoken to you since the cradle!"* She tended to get a little shrill on this point. Dad usually gave her a hug and tried to get her to another room; and *"Scholarships go to scholars!!!"* although she'd eventually dropped that one.

"Physics, the mother of billiards and other cue sports?" continued the grilling.

"Not bad. I like Physics." Joe omitted his recent amazing academic record—six F's as he'd been too stubborn to officially withdrawal. Dropping out was easier, and guaranteed to get Mom's attention if she was still out there kicking somewhere.

Gil tapped on his phone and began reading. "'Geometry is the visual study of patterns, shapes, positions and sizes.'" Joe found himself nodding. "'Jobs that require geometry...hmm, air traffic controller, construction...engineering'. A useful trade. 'Roads, tunnels—those we have—bridges, calculating volume... Sewage system design'—how does that strike you?"

"Yeah, sure. As long as I don't have to read Li.ter.a.ture." He hadn't intended to answer, but the man knew stuff. Besides, Ma would be horrified. She'd want him to study Renaissance French at the Sorbonne in Paris, or something.

The man who'd had the scrimshaw tail walked toward him. "Time for an official introduction. Joe, I'm Pete Bannerman, captain of this vessel, the fair *María Antonia Castro,* the 'Ma Castro' to her crew." He stood extending his hand. In Joe's mind's eye, his dad was making 'the face', the 'do-it-right face'. He stood and shook hand. "I'm Joe...Comstock."

"Welcome aboard." Behind the captain had come in a dozen men and women. Half the men had NFL biceps—*wasn't a ship's jail called the brig?*

"Boy's a pool player," said Gil. When he turned his head, Joe noticed a thick, dark ponytail.

"Glad to hear it." Captain Pete stirred four spoonfuls of sugar into the coffee that smelled foul and held up his hand. "Mess cook!" he shouted into the galley. A man in white tattooed to his fingertips said, "Sir?"

"Is this fresh?"

"Aye, sir. Made five minutes ago."

The captain shook his head at Gil. "Get me something better today, would you, Gil? My gut can't take it."

"Done."

"Before we speak of the game of kings, you said you're name is Comstock?" He grimaced as he sipped. He scanned a print out. "So the missing Dominic's your dad...and the lost-at-sea Anne Comstock?"

"My mom."

The captain took in the unfortunate teen before him as Gil stroked his chin and spoke. "The *Sea Wren* sank at Half Moon Bay, between San Fran and Santa Cruz."

"I remember the wave." Joe shut his eyes. "I lost her." His voice cracked. Joe fought back tears, embarrassed before the burly crewmen studying him. But the captain and Gil were being weird. "Sea WREN," said one. "SEA wren," said the other.

"Stop it! It's what my dad called my mom."

They stopped and waited.

"I'm going back to Seattle," Joe said, angrily.

"You can go anytime," said the captain. Joe gave a sideways look toward Gil. The captain shook his head. "He won't stop you. And who are you going to tell, <u>The Enquirer</u>? 'I was captured by Coast Guard Mermaids and probed!' You tell one person, kiddo, and you'll be a wacko on Twitter or whatever, for the rest of your life. Try getting into an engineering program then. Or even a pool tournament!"

Joe grabbed a bagel and went on to the top deck. Last night's deck chairs had been stowed somewhere, so he sat out of the wind beside the pilot house. *The captain's right. Whenever we get to port no one can—no one will—stop me. But where am I going without Dad's credit card? Stupid life vest. Maybe I can work a ship going north...*

The empty gray haze filled the horizon and settled in his soul. He tried not to think of The List, but it kept playing anyway: Martin, Ma, Dad, the sloop—all taken by one ocean or another.

"Young Joe." It was Doc Beautiful. "Could you possibly spare some time?"

"I'm kinda busy here, staring at the Pacific."

"Well, perhaps tomorrow."

She turned and Joe followed her like a puppy.

Chapter four

The pilothouse had five computer stations crammed into the space and a partial wall of Gorilla glass. *A crisis map.* Joe could totally imagine it all scribbled on in some emergency. "That's cool."

Melusine gave it a displeased look and turned to him. "I need you to cull the Internet for stories about people eating fish heads," she said as she got him onto a computer.

"Seriously?" She looked serious, he decided. "Like sports fishing?"

"Like this." The Yahoo News page in large bold print read: *Crazy woman rips heads off fresh fish in Japanese grocery.* "Please find any articles anywhere in the world—the computer presents everything into English, just search by country. Bookmark and keep them in a folder. Then—you can make a spread sheet? Good. Categorize by date, time, location, gender, actions, any quotes. Write that down. And I repeat, categorize by date, time, location, gender, actions, and any quotes. Also make a column of what the authorities do. Most importantly, if possible, is the type of fish, the species, Joe. And we want a follow-up section, starting for 14 separate days, and then by weeks. Leave blocks for symptoms beyond ripping fish heads. We'll talk later. I'll be looking for the Big Picture."

*Like whoa! But first...*Joe remembered the last name of the family lawyer: Miller. He'd called a few times after Dad disappeared, but Joe hadn't called back. "Attorneys Seattle Miller", he typed. *Whoa, fifteen of them! Later, dudes.* Maybe, he thought, if I build some brownie points, they'll send me home. Free.

The first story was from Vancouver—*Crazy Canadians!*—and was two days old. He formulated the spread sheet and searched. Joe scoured the <u>Vancouver Sun</u>, <u>The Province</u> and the <u>Vancouver Courier</u> and found out that Maya Chen was Canadian, 34 years old and lived in town. He found her on Facebook and Instagram. Interests: baking overly cute cookies and tango dancing and knitting hats for cats. And food choices! *Hmmm, interesting!* She went bonkers at Tokyo Market on 22 February and at 15:37 was taken by police to St. Paul's Hospital for evaluation. *"Three officers were needed to take her into custody. Two of the officers were scratched deeply."*

Joe called the Tokyo Market, the number from the Vancouver Yellow Pages. "My name is Joseph Comstock and I am an analyst with the National Oceanic and Atmospheric Administration...Yes, but we do much more than weather reports. We need to know what kind of fish the woman went after. Yes, the crazy woman...just the heads? Yes, I can wait."

Two minutes later, Joe typed in Pacific Herring. "BAM!" he said, hitting the save key. He heard clapping and turned to Melusine, Dario and some other sailors giving it up for him.

"The National Oceanic and Atmospheric Administration?" asked Melusine.

"I helped my Dad with research."

"Hmm. Might have to review those findings," she smiled.

Joe smiled back. "It gets better, Doc. The wacko girl went after Pacific Herring, locally caught. AND, on her Facebook page..."

"AND?"

"She's Vegan."

#

The Big Picture would be addressed around a small table in the Captain's stateroom, the wardroom being geared up to be the crisis center. Six chairs and the mess crew—dropping off food—filled the room, so Joe glued himself to the porthole wall, his eyes fixed on the orange sun scorching the horizon.

Almost six p.m. The last week of February.

Now, Doc B, Gil, Dario, Luz Marina, and Joe joined Captain Bannerman, who asked, "You going to pray over *this*, Gil?"

"Every time," said Gil. "One, I have to eat it. Two, I'm grateful."

"What do you call this one?" Joe asked, not recognizing the gloppy bits of white meat in library paste. It was neither French, nor Italian aka Real Food. He had a powerful yen for Mom's chicken *crapaudine*...but only if Dad were there to roll the R like Groundskeeper Willie.

"Dynamite Chicken. Fresh rats tomorrow."

"So, the Big Picture," started Melusine. "Joe, what did you find out—by the way, this young man is a decent researcher."

Joe blanked, he was still chewing a chunk of chicken. "Um...two of the four wackos—I don't what else to call them—never ate fish in their normal lives. The one in Vancouver, and the one in Chile. The fish for both were locally caught."

Melusine selected some grapes. "I am calling them 'victims'; they are victims of some causative agent. Our job is to identify it. And what were the species?"

Joe studied the spread sheet on his laptop. "Pacific herring, yellowtail tuna—"

Gil interrupted. "Yellowtails are big, eating the head would be like chewing a helmet."

Captain Bannerman said, "They can be small. Not all are game-sized."

Joe continued. "Reineta—that was Chile—and a fresh water fish called 'bagre.'"

"Fresh water?" Melusine sighed. "My major supposition that the fishes would be linked somehow is not working out."

Gil said, "You were expecting to have the same fishes from Vancouver to Chile?"

Melusine sat up straighter, lips tight. "Dario?"

"Both mercado owners said the people had super-human strength for a few hours. So they fed them all the fish heads they wanted. But after three or four hours, they both went to sleep and woke up feeling sick, like the flu."

Joe couldn't help but notice the radiant look Luz Marina gave the handsome man. Dark hair, dark brows...and his Rachel's skin. Dario continued. "Listen to this, my fellow squids. Not only was Hector Martínez Rivas a totally chilled-out dude, he was allergic to fish and shrimp!"

Captain Bannerman said, "Four people eating fish heads out of control. Two of them beyond reason. Impressive."

Luz Marina spoke. "I talked to Dr. Chester in Vancouver and he reported to me the same, but they did not give to Ms Chen any fish or fish heads. However, she swallowed a few at the beginning. She swallowed whole. Remember, she is the vegan." She shook her head and black eyes flashed. "And I received no help from San Diego! Stupid HIPAA laws—we are supposed to get information as a research branch of the government, no?"

"Therefore, at the moment we have four authenticated cases of people eating fish heads in a manic state. In a violent state." Melusine tapped her fingertips. "In all, how many people have been exposed by the primary victims?" She looked around the table. "A number, please, of secondary victims?"

"Joe came up with eight."

"Joe? Break that down, please, with injuries."

"Vancouver had like two—"

"No *like* anything. I want exact numbers."

"Okay, Doc. Two policemen were scratched and the owner was bitten pretty good on the shoulder. The San Diego dude—Zarky Jacobs, 52—was tazed after he got physical. He gave a deep scratch to the store lady. The market in Acajutlas had a brawl and four people got hurt. Two had cuts from boards and table edges in the market stalls. Marcos Hoyas Garcia, 16 years old, bit the fish vender and left his mother with a bunch of scratches. And none in Talcahuano; Dario said they just dropped fish on the sidewalk—like Hansel and Gretel—and got him to the jail. That was Victor Guevara Beltran, 35."

Dario spoke. "So six."

Melusine nodded. "Luz, do all you can to track those people. I want to keep Dario and Joe bringing in new cases. I know you will keep your own records, but please cc Joe for the flow sheet."

Luz Marina's text beeper went off. She read it and lifted her head, concerned. "Ms Chen, our first victim, has developed a high fever with chills. They will keep me informed."

"Joe, please chart that Ms Chen developed a high fever with chills at 18:23. And also the time span between eating the fish and getting the fever, which is almost three hours, correct?" Melusine nodded at the Captain who rose. "We will stay on the computers till 2200 and meet here at 0600."

After recording Ms Chen's fever, Joe went on Facebook and Twitter. *Whoa.* There was some weird stuff: crazy people raiding fish departments and biting the heads off any fish they could find. One old lady launched herself onto an iced display table, arms out sideways, grabbing smelts by the handful. *OMG!*

Back online, the sidebars did not disappoint: "10 recipes for Fish Brains", "15 ways to decorate with Fish Fins", and "Get guppy lips with plastic surgery".

After ten, Joe lay in his rack in a guest room the size of a closet, smaller that his berth on the sloop. He pulled his cap tight over his eyebrows as "Sloop John B" went through his head, the official Comstock version: "*We come on the sloop John B, Dom the Dad and me. All around Seattle town we did roam. Eating all night, Got into a fight. Well I feel so broke up, I want to go home.*" The cops had stopped looking for Dominic Joseph Comstock after two weeks, the Coast Guard after three. Joe had spent hundreds of dollars in fuel—on Dad's credit card—for the skiff, searching the dog's leg of Hood Canal, back and forth below the cliff where his car had been found—with blood on the steering wheel. Dad had been gone now for six weeks.

Here, below deck of Mermaid Central, Joe gave up. He curled around his pillow and wept for his loss.

"Rise and shine, Fuzznuts." Gil pounded on the door as he passed.

Joe, still in the same USCG sweats, rolled out of bed and over to the mess. The ship had a bit of a roll to her this morning. Filling a plate, he decided to sit next to Gil. *Either I like a challenge or I'm keeping my enemies close.* "Name's Joe, Fish Man."

The man actually smiled at that. "Naval protocol, Fuzznuts, naval protocol."

The Captain sat down and sipped his steaming cup of coffee. Another grimace.

"Umm, sir, is there like a school or anything for merms anywhere?"

"First," said Gil, intercepting. "Never use that word because we do not exist. We are 'Swimmers'. And, no, there is no Xavier Institute for X-Merms."

"Although Phelps did suggest running a summer swim camp of some sort," said the Captain.

"Phelps?!" said Joe. "Michael Phelps?"

"Heck of dolphin kick, huh?"

Joe struggled to insert the all-time best Olympic gold-medal swimmer into his DNA group, and then continued, looking at both of them. "How 'bout a sports franchise? A recording studio?"

"Slow down," said the Captain. "You're looking for some sort of "swimmer" trade school? Why? I thought Gil said you're going into civil engineering?"

"Um, just wondered."

Gil pointed his fork at Joe's nose. "You haven't finished school, have you? Thought not, sailing the coast in February."

Captain Bannerman said, "You can join the Coast Guard at seventeen—with parental consent. They will help you get the G.E.D."

"Any way around that, sir? My parents are gone. I'm sixteen April first."

"Gil can adopt you. Well, Commander?"

Joe winced. He'd seriously miscalculated that any guy with a pony tail and a camo tail should have an actual rank.

The captain looked at him intently. "So how is your pool game? You an A player?"

"They make movies about A players, sir." Joe met his eyes, straight-faced and waited. This was an interview...and not about pool. These men were elders in his tribe, Tribe HLA-B*84, a shadowy bunch who had, he suspected, a fair amount of influence. It wasn't for nothing they had a whole Coast Guard cutter to themselves! So the last thing they were about was honesty. Joe felt pretty much at home. "Just a C, sir."

A 'C' who hadn't paid for his own pizza since he was fourteen.

Chapter five

Aft, Joe paused on his way to the pilothouse, marveling at the power of the *Ma Castro*. Cap'n Pete said they could go 600 miles in 24 hours at 25 knots which wasn't even top speed. It cut effortlessly through the swells that had him holding the rail; it ignored the wind that pushed the clouds along, while the sun backlit their edges and tipped the waves with silver.

Commander Gilbert Muirgen was addressing the crew from the pilothouse as Joe entered. "All hands: we're putting in at Monterey Bay around 0900. Cook will load all his supplies dockside, while I do a Whole Foods run. The list is in the mess, if you want anything." Clicking off the intercom, he pointed at Joe. "Fuzznuts, you come with me."

Joe slipped into his computer station, hands sweating. "Are you...dropping me off, sir?" He tried not to sound scared.

"Negatory." Joe made to open his mouth. Gil said, "Need-to-know basis."

Melusine took Gil's place at the podium. "The question of the morning is 'what is special in a fish's head?' The pineal, pituitary and thyroid glands are found in fish heads. I am not, sadly, an endocrinologist, so I am consulting with Jim Sigmund at UC Davis."

A red-haired seaman spoke up. "There's a whole lot of stuff on line about the pineal gland and mysticism and shaman drugs."

"Really?" said Melusine in her most Doctor-of-Everything voice. "Please send me some credible sites."

The seaman's cheeks matched his hair.

Joe was glad he hadn't said anything. Lots of kids in Seattle got lit by grinding up and cooking down some cactus, but they usually puked. Didn't fit with the Coach's wrestling program. Anyway, all he'd read about the pineal gland had made Martin smirk. *"Pineal paranoia crap! Nooo, pinecones can't just be pinecones. Has to be a cover-up by the Vatican, no less. And the US government! Probably more fun than upgrading the highway systems."* Joe appreciated that his brother was smart. It made him believe that, sometimes, brainiacs should be in charge. But Joe wished he could sound smart once in a while. He put aside the Martin-in-his-head moment—they came unexpectedly, sometimes like cherries dropping from a tree, sometimes like bird droppings—and tried to get work done.

#

"'Good morning, Vietnam!'" said the driver taking in the magnificence of Gil in full camo glory. Joe took the back while Gil rode shotgun in the CalVets taxi van. "I see your Budweiser there, Commander. That was brown water recon."

Joe was clueless.

"Right you are. Where did you serve?"

"Missed it by two months," said the driver. "Never left the States. Man, can I say you look good for your age. You take special vitamins or something?"

"Married me a plastic surgeon," said Gil. "A fine woman. This young man needs some clothes. Some place on the way to Whole Foods."

Joe looked again at the back of Gil's head. For being a Nam Vet, he had a really thick ponytail. Not a silver rattail like his grandpa.

"Army surplus, kid? That's where I get all my gear."

"Ah...Target?"

"All righty! Here we go to Targetty-O." The driver did a Hollywood U-turn through six lanes and pulled up hard at the door of Target store.

"Outstanding!" said Gil. "Fifteen minutes, kid, full gear. This should be enough."

Joe took the three hundred-dollar bills, trying to find a pocket in the sweats without looking totally weird. A few pretty girls came out, rolled their eyes at him and looked all bored. Joe realized he couldn't remember the last time he'd been bored.

And now it's time for a shopping trip, B-Ball fans!

He grabbed a cart and started trotting to the men's department. Bam! T-shirts, long and short-sleeved, boxer briefs and socks slammed into the cart. All in ultra-cool, hide-the-grime charcoal gray. Dad told him everything had been gross-out white when he was a kid. Martin and he had done their own shopping since middle school, so Joe quickly picked out jeans, cargo shorts, and a crewneck sweater in his size. *Might have to keep the sweats, not enough cash for a decent jacket.* He paused, sadly remembering that his favorite padded flannel shirt, a skater classic, had gone down with the sloop.

Then Joe pushed the cart, skateboard style, to the shoe department and snatched some sneaks. *Man, they're half the budget. That's crazy!* After a near collision at the intersection of Seasonal and Dental Care, Joe tossed in a handful of personal products and sped to Check Out, mentally putting the short-sleeved T-shirts aside as the one thing he could do without in February.

And there—in the check-out line—it was, emblazoned on <u>The National Enquirer</u>: "FISH HEAD FEVER!" He got shoved by some rude dude with shades who was cramming his stuff almost on top of his—couldn't he wait five seconds?—so Joe reached over him and grabbed the paper and put it on top of his pile as the cashier tallied his gear.

"Might be close, just have three hundred," said Joe. The young cashier was kind of cute.

"Nah, you're good. Two ninety-six, fifty seven."

Joe handed her two chocolate bars. "Not my money," he said, grinning.

"Two ninety-nine, ninety seven." The cashier did not share his excitement, or exalt in his victory. She was all bored. Joe felt stupid...*my big stupid mouth.*

He climbed in the van and handed Gil the three cents. "Thanks, sir, and look at this." Gil—and the driver—read the headline. Gil quickly flipped the pages.

"Like Agent K says—", said the driver.

"Best investigative reporting on the planet," finished Joe.

"This is bad," said Gil. "According to *this* reporting, we are in the epicenter."

"Ahh, *man,*" said the driver. "It's gonna be Back to the Eighties. The AIDS epidemic. You remember? People didn't touch. We were afraid to share washing machines and drinking fountains. Folks going berserk over mosquito bites...might pick me up some DEET, Commander. You know, might take the old lady to Utah, to my huntin' camp. No fish for a hundred miles in any direction."

"*After* Whole Foods," said Gil. "I think it's about a half mile."

In the back seat, Joe changed into cargo shorts, a long T-shirt, nice new socks and shoes. He was thinking about his perennial big mouth. *Why'd I have to tell the cashier that it wasn't my money? I'm a total dweeb. Gil's right...I have to learn to keep my mouth shut.*

They pulled into the busy parking lot at the Whole Foods Market. Gil turned around to hand Joe a list. "You'll be doing the shopping. I'll be riding shotgun."

"What the—" said the driver, his eyes popping. "What the heck you packin'?"

Joe leaned forward to see a futuristic sub-machine gun on a strap peeking out from the flak jacket.

"A bullpup FN90, it does the job." It might have been a screwdriver for his tone of voice.

"How long is it," asked Joe.

"Sixteen inches before the nozzle's released." It was a thin shiny rectangle with curved spaces carved out for the trigger and hand grip. Was this part of being a Budweiser? He looked up to see Gil making a bored face.

"Semi-auto?" said the driver.

"Affirmative." He handed a paper to Joe. "It is now 10:15. Can you read the list? I correlated the list to the store lay-out. I want this to be a slick in-and-out."

"Do you always come armed to the grocery store?"

Gil shrugged. "Usually just the Glock in my back belt." Finally, Joe was ready and Gil instructed the driver. "You hear anything off-kilter and you meet us at the door."

"You got it!"

"Wait," said Joe. "I don't see any fancy coffee on here for Captain. I could pick up some French roast that my mom got."

"Negative. Just the items on the list."

"But you said—"

"It's never about the coffee. It's about daily battle with a worthy adversary...look, boy. The captain could have bought himself the best coffee maker and coffee in the world at any time. You are leaving that alone. Now, before my teeth fall out...March!"

Joe passed through the sliding doors...and went back seven months ago when he'd tagged along with his mom to be her bagboy. She loved the colorful, checkered display of the vegetables on the shelves. This store seemed to follow the same floor plan: first fruits and vegetables on one side, followed by fish and meats. No screaming people at fish case when they passed. Then, dairy/non dairy refrigeration along the back. Cheeses, deli and bakery went up the far side. And everything else was in the middle. "Dang sissy food," said Gil. "Plantain chips, tigernuts, dark chocolate with chilies...for the love of Pete!"

Gil insisted they go backward, against the flow, so they started at the cheese. Some of them made Joe's mouth water, Mom being a great French cook. Joe did his thing, with Gil scanning the crowd, Secret-Service style. After dropping frozen lamb chops in the cart there were just blueberries, fennel bulbs, and Japanese sweet potatoes to go. Joe pushed toward the produce, but Gil grabbed the cart, a silent finger to his lips. Something untoward was starting between the meat counter and the roots vegetables...which meant the fish counter they couldn't see.

Gil pushed him back to dairy, the edge of which was right next to the backstock area. "Go in there. I'll find you later."

But Joe stood right at the backstock entrance. Now, he could hear shouting by a number of people. "Fish heads, I want fish heads, gimme fish heads!!" Louder and faster until it was a fire-hose blast of noise. Opposing voices yelling for security and the sounds of counters being shoved, and maybe carts falling on their sides. Women began screaming and Joe could see terrified shoppers streaming to the front door, pushing their way to the outside.

Now Joe heard Gil give a loud warning, but the crazed man screamed, "I want smelts! NOOOW." Then the crazy guy was in the air, tossed by Gil into the now deserted aisle. He landed, scrambled to all fours and looked to be sniffing the air.

That's new, thought Joe.

Suddenly, Crazy Guy was screaming and rushing right at him! Gil was behind him, sailing through the air, trying to land on top of him, but the guy grabbed Joe's ankles and sank his teeth into Joe's leg as he fell forward.

Gil smashed the side of the FN90 into the guy's jaw, trying to dislodge the bite. Joe didn't scream, at first. Then, he did! And the crazy guy looked up and opened his jaws, surprised at the noise. Gil cuffed him instantly, and wrapped duct tape over his mouth and around his head for good measure.

The man screamed through the tape, kicking his feet and sweeping the floor with his legs. Gil taped his arms at his side and, last, his ankles together. Sirens sounded, and a SWAT team burst through the doors, surrounding them. "I'm calling for an ambulance," said one to Gil.

"For him," said Gil, pushing his boot against the attacker. "I'm taking my own back to the ship."

"Okay, Commander."

"Listen up, Lieutenant. Tell the medics: Full Hazmat. And close the store STAT. No one knows how this...*problem* is spread, but the "victim" here slobbered all over the fish counter. Get on the phone with whatever hospital is equipped for pandemics. Do what they say." The butcher and the SWAT team took giant steps backward.

Gil pointed to a small steak fillet in the meat case. "May I have that?" he said to the butcher. Taking it from a shaking hand, Gil slapped it onto Joe's bite, securing it with duct tape. "Clean as anything else, <u>and</u> occlusive. Now, get up, Joe. We're going back to the ship. The Doc will take care of you."

Outside, the CalVets driver was nowhere in sight. Gil shook his ponytail. "Useless."

"My clothes!" said Joe.

Gil ignored that. A car pulled up with a thirty-something young man with a crew cut. "Where can I take you, Commander?"

"Nowhere, son. Thanks. On your way."

"What?!" said Joe to the car driving away.

"Not what I wanted," said Gil, pulling out his smart phone. "Wait, here's the one!" An old man, a really old man, pulled up next to them. "Can I help you boys?"

"Well, sir," said Gil. "Not to put too fine a point on it, I need an expendable volunteer. Don't want anybody with a family depending on him, not even a dog."

"I've been alone a long time. Even the cat died. Come on in." Gil and Joe got in the musty old station wagon. Gil told him to turn right.

"You know the Coast Guard Station, about a mile down the road on Livingston?" asked Gil. The old man nodded. "Sir, this is a beaut. What is it, a '63?"

"Yep." The elderly man smiled, bunching up layers of sun-browned wrinkles and thick black splotches. "Bought her new off the lot. Had to have her, a 1963 Ford Fairlane 500 Custom Ranch Wagon. The wife eventually came around."

Joe wished he'd go a little faster. He could run a mile this fast.

"Now, what's this about being expendable?"

"This young lad was just chewed on by one of those crazy fish-head people at the Whole Foods."

"Oooh yeah, heard about that!"

"Can you stay alone for six or seven days? Don't want you out infecting anybody if we're carrying germs."

"I think I can keep the ladies away for a week. It'll hurt 'em something fierce." His chuckle turned into a thick cough.

"You're a good man, "said Gil. Reaching the dock, Gil pulled out two one-hundred dollar bills.

"No, I don't want that. I didn't do this for a reward." The driver looked offended.

"It's not a reward, sir. If you need anything delivered, here's some extra to pay for it." The man still shook his head.

"When was the last time you had this baby detailed, proper like?"

"Well..."

"Well, you're going to get it detailed because the United States Coast Guard is in your debt." Gil transferred the bills as part of a handshake. "Or give it to the nuns. God bless you, sir."

Fighting back tears, the old man said, "God bless you, too, son."

Chapter six

"Why was he crying?"

"I reckon he's had a whole lot of nothing lately."

Joe didn't feel good and started to sway; Gil swung him up in his arms like a sack of laundry. "Confirm Doc's on her way to sickbay," he said as he strode past the security officer atop the boardwalk.

She was. Standing cross-armed, glaring. "What. Happened?"

"The 'victim'", Gil said with thick sarcasm, "bit the boy."

"God help us all. Young Joe, you just can't stay out of my sickbay..." He watched her put on a gown and gloves and mask. "Because I'm so pretty."

"Yes, ma'am." Melusine became all Dr Vidmorya and pointed to the exam table. Joe sat.

"Why is there a forty-dollar fillet mignon on your leg?"

"Gil said it was clean."

"In Nam," said Gil, unfazed by her professional scorn, "we used leaches and maggots too, like the Blackfoot." An all-man alarm pierced the air. Gil took off running.

"Gil is somewhat prehistoric in his medical preferences." She gave a tssk. "And duct tape on a hairy leg. On three," she said. She pulled on two as Joe yelped. "Hmm. When was your last tetanus shot?"

"Two years ago."

"Swear to God?"

"Yeah, before an alleged family vacation. To Europe." He watched her head tilt side to side. "Am I going to die?"

"You know what I know. We are still accumulating our information on primary victims, much less the secondary. That's what you are, a secondary victim. I am going to give you the appropriate antibiotics for the wound—human mouths are notoriously filthy. Give me a dog bite any day—and you are going into isolation." She smiled. "We will do everything we can. And I expect you to keep on researching; you can use that laptop."

Joe took a deep breath. "I'm hungry." Melusine looked him askance. "No fish," he said. "Toasted cheese."

Two breaths later, they heard shots. "That is ordnance! Now what? This was supposed to be a routine reload." As she spoke, Melusine rubbed a sterile culture swab over the bite, going in a bit deep in parts, he thought with a grimace.

Dario walked into the sickbay, followed by Gil. Dario was gray, all the brightness gone from his face. Gil spoke. "I shot the perp. After he gouged Dario, I shot him just to stop him. What do we do with him?"

"With Dario? He sits on the exam table. Joe, move to the chair," directed the doctor. "And the one you shot...I presume he's dead."

"Maybe." Melusine and Gil looked at each other steadily until Gil picked up the desk phone. "Commander Muirgen here, please call the captain to sickbay, Stat."

Melusine shook her head and repeated the ministrations done to Joe. "Last tetanus?"

"Eight years ago."

"We will repeat that. Do you know where Luz Marina is?"

Dario looked more stricken, if possible. "She went for a swim, ma'am. You know how she loves the Bay."

Melusine removed her gloves and scrubbed her hands vigorously to the elbow at the sink with foot peddle controls. "Lie down on the table for now, Dario; we will be next door. Your isolation starts now. Speakers shall be left on."

Joe and Dario stood frozen next to the speaker as Captain Bannerman listened to Gil's account of the two attacks. He called into the sickbay; "Seaman, any idea what provoked the attack?"

Dario answered. "We were offloading boxes of frozen fish, sir. He stuck his nose to the boxes and just went off!"

"My guy, too!" said Joe. "He sniffed the air like a dog and then charged right at me, like, like I was a giant fish head." To that, Melusine reviewed the little that was known and the problem of the injured/dead man below.

"Well," said the captain, "if we keep the injured man—he's not dead as of now and the medics are being careful—we risk further contamination onboard. I'd rather not. Can we safely isolate Dario and Joe? In case?"

"Barely. They are best kept here. Between Luz Marina and myself, we will identify the causative agent first, I am sure. We do not think it is airborne...nor do we know for certain. The spread by body fluids is our acting hypothesis.

"Sickbay is portside," said the captain. "Keep all port windows closed?"

Melusine nodded. "Except these scuttles. They need air."

"Supplies stowed, Pete?" Gil asked.

"Yes," said the captain. "We can sail. Or not. This is uncharted territory and maybe we just stay put. What we can do is med-evac this goober to the VA in San Fran. Gil, can you start that or does Doc initiate?"

"Got it," said Gil.

"Either way, we wait for Luz," said Melusine. "And we wait for the Director who is currently en route."

Wearing full hazmat gear, Dr Melusine Vidmorya efficiently rearranged the sickbay while the possibly infected sat behind a curtain. Two laptops were placed so they could work. A cot on wheels was locked in place for a second bunk. "If you start attacking each other, gentlemen, this arrangement won't work." She hung two clipboards with schedules for temperature and antibiotics; she provided thermometers and pills. Linens were stored in the head with soap. "No shower. Sorry, but the sink in here has potable water." She paused. "Food...that will be canned or bottled fruit or juices, cereals, bread, cheese. PB and J, hardboiled eggs."

"Not the eggs, ma'am," said Dario. Joe agreed. "They're peeled and packed and don't roll. We'll make do with the rest. Won't be long, will it, ma'am?"

Melusine smiled and tipped her head; Joe figured that was her evasive motion. She continued. "Here is the first aid kit. You will be assisting each other. Now, about work. I am relieving you of hunting for new victims and the spread sheet of progressive symptoms. I will add that 'sniffing the air' behavior, by the way. Instead, I want you to call the families of the victims—the primary victims—and get the most detailed and current information you possibly can on what they have eaten in the last 48 hours. At least get that, although a thorough history of their diet choices would be best.

"Take your first temperatures at 2, then 6 and 10 tonight. Start the same in the AM. If you can work till 7 or 8 tonight, it would be most appreciated." Melusine MD left.

At this moment, Joe imagined arm-wrestling Martin for the bunk. He exhaled, hating the slice-like-a-knife feeling of family memories, and opened his laptop. He brought up the spread sheet and split the screen...and called the sister of Miss Vancouver, Maya Chen.

"...so your sister never eats dairy—except milk chocolate—and her favorite vegetable is bok choy...AND baby carrots with spinach dip." He repeated as he tapped the template. "But spinach *soy* dip, right? Not dairy. She just doesn't drink white milk—because she's a Vegan. Right...Except chocolate milk, and half-and-half in her tea." *Note to self: don't be a nutritionist.* "What else does she like to drink? Why? Um, well ma'am, we couldn't find a fish in common that the first four people who got sick ate, so we're looking for something they all might have eaten. Okay, thank you. Sweet tea, Sierra Mist. Water? Bottled. What was the last meal you saw her eat: Breakfast, granola bar with chocolate chips and she usually buys coffee on the way to work.

"So no meats? Just chicken when Mom makes it and tea eggs and peanut butter? Okay. Loves Triskets. And pork lo mein. Is there a vegan type? Not for Chinese New Year. Thank you. (He said "thank you" only because Melusine had printed in "thank you" at regular intervals in script she wanted him to use. *Ohhhh, Doc. How annoying can people be?*) "Seafood," he continued, "loves shrimp, but not eating it now," he said along with the sister, "because she's Vegan. Fried foods: potato chips, French fries, sweet potato fries. Fried ramens. Would you say she prefers Chinese food to the Standard American Diet? (*Another Melusine phrase.*) Thanks...any other foods not on this list? Wine. Red wine, kelp noodles...and tiramisu. Thank you very much for your time. Goodbye."

Joe zoned out, staring at an illustration on the wall, *Tomba della Sirena*. Appropriate. An old pen-and-ink rendering showing a twin-tailed mermaid flanked by winged guards. The tails' length was heaped and folded on the ledge above the tomb and the whole thing was carved into the side of a large stone cave somewhere.

Dario looked up from his interview in Spanish, touching his fingers to his lips as though eating delicacies. Joe pretended to bang his head on the wall.

Mess crew delivered the food boxes to the door. "There are Girl Scout cookies in there, bro," said one. "Keep the faith, dudes," said the other.

Dario hung up. "Next vacation might be to Chile. Those people know how to eat!"

"Miss Vancouver doesn't. She's a dedicated almost, kinda Vegan."

Dario smiled. "And it's fourteen hundred hours." He put his thermometer in his mouth and recorded it. Joe did the same. Dario's was 98.9. Joe's was 99.1. He turned the clipboards to the glass wall, so Melusine could see them...and he couldn't.

"This is important, right?" said Joe, indicating the laptop.

"Gotta find the link." Loud voices, high and low, were coming quickly towards them. "She's back," said Dario.

"*Mi vida, mi vida!*" Luz Marina's hands were desperate starfish on the glass, her face a mask of fear.

"You can't go in, Luz." Gil gently edged her away from the door.

Dario put his hand on the glass over hers. "I'm okay, *mamita*. *No te preocupes*. I'm fine. Me and Joey are just hanging out. It got too crowded to work up top."

"His temperature's normal." Melusine pointed to the clipboards.

"Drink water, *mi amor*, lots of water!"

"And Girl Scouts cookies, eh Joey?" Dario opened the box and munched on a cookie. "The scratches were like nothing. Doc just went over the top, you know, like she does." Joe thought the scratches were more like something, but he nodded and took a thin mint. Dario looked at Melusine. "We're not making much progress on these food habits. Maybe she could help?"

Luz Marina seemed to steady herself and stood taller. She made her work station in the lab with a window facing their space. After four hours, she stood with Melusine at the glass window comparing notes. "Anything interesting?" asked Melusine.

"People eat crap," said Joe. "And I'd still like a beer. Organic if you've got it."

Ignoring him, Luz Marina told of the three people she had interviewed in San Diego and two people in El Salvador. And she had added in Joe's and Dario's work: "Both the North American victims take antacids, the South Americans use peppermint tea for upset. San Diego takes a statin and is allergic to Rapaflo. Vancouver is allergic to penicillin, Chile is allergic to fish and shrimp. El Salvador eats a simple diet—rather starved—and thinks ice cream is the best thing in the life."

Melusine said, "Did Beltran in Chile have an allergic reaction to the fish?"

Dario answered. "He got a rash, an itchy rash. They gave him Benadryl and it went away." Melusine nodded, standing there with Luz Marina waiting for the 6 pm temperatures.

Dario shook his head. "Our temps are like the Easter Bunny. You can't watch. Take a hike!" After a staring war, they left. "Joe, can you heat me a burrito. Man, I'm bushed. Got a headache...99.3."

"Drink more water. " Joe looked at list on the clipboard. "Says 'target or rash'."

Dario made a mean-guy face. "Lift your shirt, dude. Turn around. Eww, what's that?" Joe felt his all his blood drop below his heart. Dario continued. "My cousin had a target like that. His doc said it was Lyme's. Me?" Dario lifted his shirt and turned slowly around.

"Nada," said Joe, checking the 6 pm column, and took his own temp. "Same, 99.3."

Chapter seven

Joe sat in the dark, thinking about his family—Martin, his smart talented brother. Every teacher who ever had Martin found Joe a disappointment. But he'd adored him, would have given body parts for him. Ma—fussy, demanding, made the greatest food and wanted him to *be* something...ahh, it was so easy to push her buttons. And Dom the Dad. Best dad ever. Nice, funny.

Boy, was I stupid. I thought I could sail away from missing them. A deep sigh came from his belly and a headline flashed through his brain: Last of the Comstock Line Dies from Fever.

Didn't see that coming.

Dario turned in his bunk, moaning. Joe wondered if he were an only child too—Joe's unwelcomed position as of a year ago. And, suddenly, an orphan. Just odd, he thought, that families could dwindle to nothing in a year. Joe found himself whispering to the computer screen. "Here's the funny thing, the really hilarious thing: I got rescued for THIS! Yesterday I thought I would repair the sloop, go home and rescue the dog from old Mrs. Lauder, maybe even fix Commander Fish Man's sewers..."

Slow down, boy, it's just a fever. A Martin-in-his-head moment. *Right, time to chill...for real!*

A small LED light on the bunk allowed him to see that Dario was grimacing in his sleep. Perhaps Dario was smart going to bed early, but it made Joe nervous.

*It's not right; he and Luz Marina love each other. At least, nobody will miss me...*and BAM, Joe was staring at his bucket list, the bucket list he was too young to have: *going to the Prom with Rachel.* "Stupid," he whispered to himself. "You gave that up months ago; you said proms were so lame. Maybe I should call her...and say "Hi Rache. Yeah, sorry. I should have called, but I've been like sailing down the coast and trying pretty hard to drown. No, I'm okay, just like I'm possibly dying and might take out some people while screaming for fish heads... Yeah, first on the block!"

I need a different bucket. Okay, try again: sail round the world, date a hot redhead, race a penny-farthing, jump a train, ride a real bronco and make it to six-foot.

He tried hard to care about the sunken sloop. All Joe really wanted was a lower temperature at 10 pm.

The light lingered in the western sky. The portside of the cutter, docked on the curve of Monterey Bay, faced a beach. With the fading light in the western sky, Joe could see people at the water's edge and wished to be with them...or did he? He'd been shown the moveable telescope with video cam mounted to the deck. It connected to the laptop. He turned it on and zoomed in. The happy people on the beach were an angry mob. "Commander Gil," he said into the intercom. "You gotta see this." And as he waited, a dozen people started beating one man with whatever weapons they had brought.

Gil called back.

"Sir, there's badness on the beach. Yeah, port through the tele-cam...oh no, they just killed him!"

"Roger that," said Gil. Joe and Gil separately watched three men toss the new corpse into the water. He floated, head down, without resistance. The gang or ten or twelve stood and watched.

"Sir, do you think he was like a victim? I mean of the fish thing?"

"Unknown. More likely a rival gang member." The crowd seemed to have brought beer and they stood around drinking. Joe could hear Gil giving orders to one of his security minions as he watched someone put a match to papers in a wire trash can. Like a regular party, some men started on their second beer.

"Having a good time," said Gil. "Out in the water—look, boy!" As they watched, the newly dead put his feet down in the water and lifted his head. And turned to his murders. Staggering slightly, he ran into their midst attacking them with great strength. "Rewind it, son. Tell me exactly how long the dead man had his face down in the water. I'll keep watching ...Joe? Do you roger?"

Joe heard Gil page the captain and Dr Vidmorya as he hit rewind and fast forward. "Joe? How long?"

"He floated for eight minutes and fourteen seconds....Sir?"

"What?"

"Um, nothing." *Come hold my hand? Tell me there are no monsters under the bed?* Joe held his tongue.

"Over and out."

He continued staring at the telecam. Nothing to see now. Everyone—including the whatever-it-was—was gone. *Whaddya mean "the whatever-it-was"? Don't be such a freakin' girl. That was a ZOMBIE! The Walking Dead. A corpse come back to life without divine intervention.* Joe closed the laptop gently, and stood at the portal window. He knew he would type in the news or link to *Walking Dead* episodes if he stayed seated.

"Hey, Martin," he whispered into the dark night. "I'm feeling your 'broad brush of irony' here. Forget just being gross and attacking people for fish heads. No, I get the chance to be a zombie. I win, dude!"

Joe pressed on his eyeballs; pushing against the stabbing pain behind them. *I do not have a headache; I do not have a headache...because if I do have a headache, then I have THE headache.* He put his head between his hands. He had a target, he had a temperature and now his head hurt. This was not good.

"Young Joe." It was Melusine on the speakerphone. "How are you doing? I see you have a target on your back."

"Freakin' great, Doc."

"Take your temperature and I'll give you an update."

"I don't want to."

"I'd like you to...how do you feel?"

"I see a ba-ad moon risin'" he sang, twanging an air guitar. "I see trouble on the way. I see—"

"Do you need a sleeping pill? There's Benedryl in the med box."

"That's got to be the dead-stupidest thing anyone's ever said to me. A sleeping pill?! I might be dying and you're giving me a sleeping pill?"

"Wait," she said with some energy. "Tell me the magnificent leap of intellect you have taken to go from a fever of unknown origin to dying."

"Don't leave out the fun of becoming the Undead." He returned to singing. "Well don't go around tonight...it's bound to take your life, there's a bad moon on the rise."

"Shh. Don't wake Dario. "

"What are you doing about the zombie?"

"The MPs are working with the Carmel police. You may think you're going to die, but I'm not going there with you. We have absolutely no evidence linking this oddness to the fevers. Remember: Correlation does not imply causation. Am I clear?"

Joe didn't answer, because now he knew what to put on his bucket list: not to become a zombie...he looked at his bunkmate. And not being around if Dario did.

#

The murder on the beach made it into the morning shows and headlines, actually. "FISH HEAD FEVER—ZOMBIE LINK?" And "GUN SALES SPIKE."

"Spike!" said Melusine at the sickbay desk. "Don't we already have enough guns for every man, woman and child in this country?"

"Try two," said Gil.

"Next will be the machete," said Luz Marina.

"Nope, too short a reach, *mujer*."

Dario and Joe had been up since 0600 hours, Luz Marina, Gil and Melusine staring in as they took their temps. Joe still had a headache and muscle aches, just like the flu. The target was still there and his temp was an even 100. Dario had no target. His headache was terrific, muscle aches were minor and he had a hard time buttoning his shirt. His temp was 100.8

"Doc B, I mean Vidmorya—any chance of some fish heads? It's crazy. I could eat them raw."

"Same here," said Dario. "All right, the freak show is closed till noon." They sat with their backs to the window. "Doc B?"

"Yeah," said Joe. "B like Beautiful."

"Roger that," said Dario. "We're doing great, right, buddy?"

"Roger that," said Joe.

Later, a tray came through the door. "Fresh ones courtesy of Commander Muirgen." Four small plates, two with fresh smelts, two with fried oval surf perch. "Holy crap, that's good!"

Dario said something short in Spanish as he guzzled his. They noticed Melusine and Luz Marina at the window. "Best food ever!" said Joe.

"Fascinating," said "Doc B". "What exactly do you crave? The fillets? Just the heads?

"It's the brains, ma'am," said Dario. "I want to suck them out like marrow. But the smelts are so small, I just bite 'em off." Joe lifted a "thumbs-up" with his mouth stuffed.

"More?" said Luz Marina. "What would you like, *mi vida*?"

"Well, if you're going "shopping", I love the herring best."

"I saw some yesterday, *mi rey. Hasta pronto*."

"Wow," said Joe. "She's great." Dario nodded. Joe didn't know if it meant anything, but Luz Marina's hair wasn't as curly. *A "swimmer" thing?*

Doc B tapped the window. "Please let me know if, when or how you feel satiety, fullness. And put everything—plates, fish remains—in the red plastic bags. To be incinerated later."

"Could I, may I have a beer?' said Joe.

"No. Beer has active yeast. I am trying to limit infectious factors here."

"I might be dying and I can't have a beer?!" Joe gave his best Bambi look to Gil who just joined the window watchers.

"Boy's got a point," said Gil.

"As do I." Melusine tilted her chin down and stared at Joe. "When you are actively dying, you may have a beer. But today's choices are bottled juices or Mexican Coke."

#

Alone for a moment, Joe typed up notes while Dario rested his head on his hands.

Totally dead boring. Mr. Jacobs, aka San Diego, loved cheese and spaghetti, said his wife. At least, she could think in a straight line. His headache had lessened and Gil had rigged sound from the crisis center to the sickbay with a volume control. Joe felt better with the low-level noise and busy-ness of the phone calls and discussions, the cable and satellite feeds. He was checking "flu-like symptoms resolving" on Day 3 when he heard:

"Whoa! Look, sir. That's Burbank, Johnny Carson Park. I grew up near there."

"What station?" shouted Dario to the intercom.

"KCET." He and Dario got it on screen in time to see a young mother shooting a man in the chest at two paces.

"No blood," said Commander Gilbert Muirgen, head of ship security, from the crisis center. As they watched, she fired a shot each to his knee caps. "She's military. Following protocol!"

The dead person continued to move forward, crawling on his stomach with his elbows. "Zombies!" people began to shout. "He's a zombie!" Families frantically gathered their children who were screaming for their pets. "Is that a rat in the cage?" asked Dario of a cage just to the left of the shooter's foot.

She fired two more rounds. Right shoulder. Left shoulder. "Now the head shot, young lady," Gil said.

Joe had to close his mouth to talk. "He's still pushing with his toes!"

She put the pistol at the ear nearest her and fired, then one above the eye. Clean shots that extruded splattered brain on the ground. As the young mother glanced at her babies in their stroller, 8 rounds spent, the dead man grabbed her foot and ankle, raking open the skin.

Everyone in the crisis center groaned.

Captain Bannerman said, "I need that broadcast from the beginning."

"Aye sir. This is the noon news. Annnd running..."

"Hi, I'm Sandi Selino here in Johnny Carson Park, Burbank, for the second annual Fun Festival and Pignic. 'Cavies' are, for the uninformed, guinea pigs that originated in the Andes and are close relatives to the Capybara, the world's largest rodent and star of urban legends. And while the cavies here today do not have their cousins with them, we have many families here to celebrate the joy of Guinea Pigs as their family members. Let's hear from Miss Magnolia Poindexter."

"Yes, we here at CavyYard are dedicated to helping families decide if they would like to share their homes with one of our little cavies. And we mean 'home'. Our little darlings love to be in the middle of the action."

"No cages?" said the reporter.

"What's wrong with a dog?" The guys in sickbay heard Gil interject.

"We offer them protective areas as one would have for a cat, for example a hotel with a scratching post."

"Would my cat like one?"

Joe and Dario heard snickers from the crisis center as Miss Poindexter shot Sandi an evil look. "I mean, can cats and cavies coexist?" That interview ended awkwardly and Sandi Selino stooped to ask a very young girl about her brown and white cavies. "This one's name is Cimmamim, and the white one is Wice Cake, and Cimmamim peed on Daddy today, and Daddy said—"

"Thank you! This is Sandi Selino, KCET, Burbank. Let's go down to this tent where the costume contest will take place in a few minutes." Eager children happily thrust their pets into the camera's way. One guinea pig sported a fringed leather vest with a feather in its beaded headband, another was a green Stegosaurus with red felt points running down its spine, and a third was dainty fairy ballerina swathed in tulle.

At that point, the cameraman followed the noise of shouting, the young mother yelling at a man who looked if he had finished a long run through mud and was exhausted.

"Get away from my children!" The man lumbered toward her two babies in the stroller, arms outstretched. Their mother stepped in front of it and pulled a small pistol from a vest pocket. "I have a gun and I will shoot." She shot him in the left chest.

He advanced.

"Glock 27," said Gil as they watched the shootings a second time.

"That's classic Zombie!" said a seaman.

"It's classic nothing!" said Melusine. "A staggering walk followed by being shot is not the same as eating brains. I assume that's your line of thought."

"How do you explain the apparent 'deadness' of the man who kept moving?" said the Captain.

"I don't, I can't. I'm a scientist. I need cause and effect. I need *repeatable* cause and effect."

"Oh no!" All turned to the screen. A lumpy fifty-some woman was pulling an infant from a vibrating infant seat on a table. "She's gonna bite it!" said Dario as the probable mother punched her in the jaw and another woman put her scarf around her neck and pulled. The baby screamed shrilly, a bad sound. Two more women with the same staggering gate were coming from the east side of the park. No more guns came out of hiding as parents and children fled, leaving their pets.

"Let's get out of here, NOW," said Sandi to her cameraman.

"Look," he said. The TV screen showed all three women extracting squealing guinea pigs from cages and trying to push them in their mouths. "Move! We're done here, sister." The screen went black.

"And we assume they had their snacks," said the captain.

"Make an honest sandwich, one of them. But the brains...not even a slider."

"That has to be Red," said Dario, listening and shaking his head.

"Missing persons!" said Melusine. "We've not wondered about missing persons! That's what *they* are. The ones that contracted the fevers *un*associated with fish markets! God in heaven, we need samples!"

"What *have* they been eating?" said Luz Marina. "We look for not just fish!"

Next, they heard Gil ordering his next-in-command to call Animal Care. "LAPD. See what's going on—pets lost, animals found mutilated. Things they might attribute to coyotes or wolves." Followed by: "Who's the victim? The man full of bullets, idiot."

"Is he talking to the cops?!" Joe said, trying to keep up.

"The Commander knows everyone," said Dario. "In every port."

Gil addressed the crisis center. "Listen up, gang: LAPD doesn't know the dead man; they'll post photos on the news and social media and Missing Persons for him and the three hungry females."

"The shooter?"

"One Sarah Bruno, a recently discharged Army Corporal and MP. Smart cookie. She realized no blood meant something."

"The guy could have been out running and collapsed and died."

"So, Red, that's why you don't run," yelled Dario back into the speaker.

"I'm waiting for you, dude," said Red.

"We'll be running the paint off the deck when I'm back, buddy!"

Chapter eight

Melusine sat down in the tiny lab of sickbay. She punched numbers into the phone. "This is Dr. Vidmorya of the Coast Guard. We have two active cases of—I do not use that term, but it will do. We are collecting samples. Could you put aside...you will not? This could be bigger than Ebola and we have no backlog on our DNA or chromospectometer—"

They watched her stare at the receiver in her hand. "Stupid insolent pig!"

She punched in another number. "Lucas, Melusine here. A victim was shot down in Johnny Carson Park—you saw it? I need stomach contents and intestinal track and urine and blood and CSF...Yes, well, they are being absolute fools! I told them we had DNA testing with no backlog. Yes, I will take the whole body...that was sarcasm? This may be worse than Ebola and you're being sarcastic?! Lucas, I am looking at two crewmen sick with it as I speak. And I am also concerned about the wound on the woman who shot him. Could you at least send an oral swab...thank God for that! She has two children...Do you have her telephone number? Yes I will take it. I will call her, and tell her to report to UCLA Medical Center under your service. Correct. Lucas, thank you."

She stood for this phone call, resting her hip on the desk. "Hello, Ms Bruno? No, I am not a reporter. I am a physician, Dr. Vidmorya of the Monterey Bay Coast Guard. First, may I commend you on your brilliant assessment of the situation and quick actions. We have been following active cases of this disease from Canada to Chile. The one person who was *scratched*, as you were, survived after barely sickening. It seems to be different when people are bitten."

Melusine realized Joe and Dario had heard her and she frowned. "My comrade, Dr Lucas Casas at UCLA Medical Center, will take you as a patient. It will be in the protective isolation suite where they would keep Ebola patients, therefore the best care. He will be analyzing what is in your wounds and what was on the—zombie, if that's what you call him." She smiled. "I know you will. So you will go? Excellent. Yes, they are waiting for you...You are very welcome."

She put the phone in its cradle and spoke at Joe and Dario. "This will go far to dismiss insect bites and pollutants. Ms. Bruno will be our third witnessed infected case. Time?"

"15:23," said Joe.

When she was out of sight, Dario shoved his laptop to the wall. "You're doing okay, Joey?"

"I think so."

"Come over here." When he got there, Dario began to whisper. "I can't type, dude, my fingers don't work. I don't think I'm going to make it." Joe began to protest, but Dario bumped him with his elbow. "Stop. You were sick, now you're better. I'm getting worse. I walk like Frankenstein. I'm blanking out—some sort of seizures. I can't tell La Luz and Doc won't stop trying, but we need to be ready. Know what I mean?"

Joe glanced at the window where Luz Marina had come to keep her vigil. Her hair seemed straighter today than it had been yesterday, and thinner. He turned and looked out the porthole, trying to ignore Dario.

"Joey," whispered Dario. "*Joey.* Promise me you will cut my head off. As soon as I die, as soon the ECG flat-lines, cut my head off. There's got to be a scalpel around here."

Joe whispered back, "Doc B says there's no proof there's a connection between the guy reanimating and the fish head fever."

A chorus of groans from the crisis center had Joe turning up the volume. Maya Chen had just died in Vancouver General Hospital.

"Válgame, Dios!" Luz Marina collapsed on her arms and wept until she shook. Gil came in and stood behind her, resting his hands on her shoulders. Slowly she turned and cried onto his stomach.

"Guess we'll see, Joey."

Joe whispered back through his teeth, "Dead is only dead. It's not zombie!"

"Right," said Dario with grim sarcasm. "That's what the Pignic was all about."

Joe texted a request to Melusine for Maya Chen's records. *Why?* "I want to know if she got violent at the end." A few minutes later, *Yes, she did.* "Could Luz Marina go someplace else? She's not helping matters."

Even as we speak. As Joe looked through the glass, Gil was carrying the still sobbing Luz Marina out of the lab.

Dario fell onto the cot. "Wait," said Joe, "you have the bunk."

"Well, I want the cot now. Joey, the straps will be easier on the cot."

"Will you stop!? She died, all she did was die."

"Let's have a beer."

Joe typed Melusine, again. "We're both ready for our beer."

Reply: "*Coming.*"

Minutes later, in hazmat gear, Melusine came into the lab with two chilled bottles: one Dos Equis and one Coke. Joe frowned in frustration; he twisted open the beer and handed it to Dario. He sat, spent, too drained to open his own.

"Dario," said Melusine, "I want you to hear this from me and not the Internet. Maya Chen reanimated."

Dario stared at the floor.

Joe stood up. "How do you know she wasn't just in a coma?"

"She was dead, Joseph."

"You know for sure?"

"I do."

"How?" Joe persisted.

"I know that she was dead for sure because the coroner was weighing her heart on the scale."

Joe sat down, his hands tight around the Coke. Dario said, "Did she attack?"

"Yes. They shot out her brain stem and now she is truly gone." She and Dario sat in silence. He spoke. "I need to see the Commander."

She nodded. "I shall send him. Want to see the padre as well?"

Dario nodded.

When they were alone, Dario said, "Joey. Tell la Luz that I love her very much."

"She's really nice," said Joe, knowing that was the lamest thing he had ever said, but couldn't think of anything else.

"Tell her later, after." Joe helped Dario lie down. His one leg was off the cot, twitching. "Dios mio, I'm hot."

Gil was on the sickbay phone. Joe said, "It can't wait, sir. He's bad."

"Tell him I'm bringing ratchet straps," said Gil. "The ones we use to secure machinery in the hold. Get him on the stretcher that you were sleeping on. More control than the bunk bed." Joe was very glad Dario was already on the stretcher. He pushed the red foot pedals to the lock position, just to make sure.

A knock on the door was the priest. Joe listened to Dario's confession, and to the priest's absolution: "Fear not those who kill the body but are powerless to kill the soul." Dario mouthed the words of the Creed. ". . . and we believe in the resurrection of the dead and the life of the world to come." But in the middle of the Our Father, Dario bent at the middle, convulsing. With effort, he laid back on the stretcher, breathing heavily. The priest finished the prayer, "...deliver us from evil. Amen." Luz Marina slipped in and gripped Dario's hand. She looked like an ancient mourning Madonna with tears streaming from her large eyes.

The priest continued, making the Sign of the Cross upon his forehead. "May the Lord Jesus protect you and lead you to eternal life."

The priest left and Gil called to Joe at the door. He was all business and tense. "Here, start putting these on. The end goes through the loop. Tight. Ankles, above the knee, across the hips—Luz Marina, don't make me come get you—chest with arms at the biceps and forehead. Now!"

Joe started at the ankles. The straps were strips of metallic bumps melted on woven nylon to resist the buckle from loosening. "Now above the knees." Gil called from the door, "Dario, buddy, put your hands at your side. Perfect."

Luz Marina held his face. "Oh!" She felt his forehead and framed his face in her hands. "You are steaming hot." She kissed his forehead.

Dario tried to smile. "I'm Latino...no, no crying, mamita."

"Joe, escort her to the door, NOW," said Gil. "Luz Marina, come here. Dario doesn't want to hurt anyone and he might get violent."

Joe pushed against her, but she resisted. "Please," he begged her. "He doesn't want to hurt anybody. Please."

She weakened and Joe pulled her to Gil's waiting hands. "Quickly, Joe. Now the one across the chest at the nipple line and around his biceps. That's right, tighten the strap. Work fast. Pull it! See that half block of memory foam with the center carved out? Dario, ready for your head?" Dario was beginning to thrash. "Get *behind* him, kid. Across the forehead and tighten it below. One more, across the hips, securing his forearms."

"Put the pulse ox on his finger," urged Melusine from the lab. "Push the ON button." Dario blinked rapidly and seemed to be in another place. He began to buck the straps and call out odd phrases in English and Spanish.

Joe struggled to secure the probe as Dario's hands waved and clenched.

"That was too close," said Gil.

With the pulse oximeter light on, Joe asked, "Do I have to stay in here?"

"I am not certain," said Melusine. "I believe you have immunity now, but I cannot guarantee that you are not contagious...if you say so, Director. All right, Joe, put your laptop in a red biohazard bag so we can clean it and keep it operating. Just scrub your hands up to the elbows, mask, and then come out."

All the while Dario continued to buck his restraints which held, but the cot stood four feet high and Joe worried it could topple. He pushed the desk in front of the cot to secure it against the wall. Then, he scrubbed and escaped the deathbay.

And looked into the face of his mother.

Chapter nine

"Ma?!"

"My 'eart beats again!" She stood with her arms outstretched, welcoming him, but Joe's feet would not move. "I am relieved beyond words that you 'ave recovered, *mon grand*."

He did a half-pivot away, turned his head and said, "Whatever."

He headed for the ladder well. Up top, the ocean was still, but Joe shambled listlessly like the Undead.

She didn't tell us. He ripped off his mask and gripped the rail. *She didn't tell Dad!* His blood roiled with anger, boiled with resentment. *Like what does it take to text "I'm fine, see you later"? Obviously, obviously*—Joe struggled to let out a thought that hurt him more than the day-to-day pain of her being gone, *we just didn't count. She let me think she was dead...that I had nobody. Who does that to their kid?!*

The perfect afternoon, complete with a gentle salty breeze and the warm early-spring sun, was wasted on him. He had a mother; she was below...but Joe wanted nothing to do with her. *I threw away my junior year!* Joe slid down the pilot house exterior and sank to the deck, a pile of leaden remorse. *We could have searched for Dad together.* The sun was close to the water line when the odd sound of a brass bell sounding penetrated his particular misery. The usual electronic oscillating alarm had sounded a bit ago, but this was metal on metal. *Ding, ding. Ding, ding. Ding, ding. Ding, ding.* Eight bells. End of the watch?

Shortly after, the Captain spoke on the intercom. "Bravo Zulu, Seaman Dario Garcia Cabrillo. Well done. The crew and I extend our deepest condolences to his devoted mother, Doctora Luz Marina Cabrillo."

His mother!? Not his girlfriend? Joe put his head back and blew out air. *Something else I got wrong.* He decided on a shower, that couldn't go too wrong. *At least Dario had had a nice mom—devoted, catching his favorite fish...She didn't mess up his life.*

Below deck, he walked along the bulkhead and heard his mother berating some unfortunate in French, a language he had heard all his life but refused to speak. She accused him of gross stupidity for putting her son in danger. It was Gil that answered, in French! He did not defend himself. Joe nodded as Gil mostly agreed with "the Director"—always the best tack with his mom—and the one he personally had used the least.

Joe zipped into his tiny guest quarters, unseen. He showered long and scrubbed hard, but it did not lessen the betrayal he felt—that dog kept on biting. He shaved what he had and brushed his teeth and combed his hair, but still the sharp spikes of rejection poked him and the thorns of doubt pressed in.

Abandoned. That's the word you're looking for. Martin-in-his-head to the rescue.

He put on a clean set of USCG sweats. Dom the Dad filled his mind and the question that he so often had asked: "What have we learned today, son?"

Mostly, Joe decided, that he didn't know much, wasn't worth much, guessed wrong and made bad decisions whenever possible...and that he shouldn't want a beer at this time, but he really did. Pity about the Dos Equis...

There was one question he did want to ask his mother.

He walked back to the captain's stateroom –she obviously outranked Cap'n Pete. Now she was speaking Spanish. More new stuff!

"Ma," Joe said, at the doorway.

"Oui?" She sat with her arms around Luz Marina who was wrapped in a blanket. Most of her wild chestnut hair had fallen out and the parts of her tail he could see were blotchy and dull. Luz Marina looked at him, too. He recognized those miserable eyes; he'd seen the same ones in the mirror for months.

"I'm really sorry, Luz Marina." She nodded, barely. "He, um, Dario said...he made me promise to tell you...after...that he really loved you. I thought you were—I didn't know you were his mother." *Stop talking, fool.*

Both women sat quietly, looking at him. Finally, his mother spoke. "We are leaving soon. Luz Marina needs the sea."

Joe found his nerve. "Were you even on that plane?" His anger boiled. "Why the crap are you smiling?"

"I was on that plane," she said. "And I smile because Martin never would 'ave doubted me. Our noble Martin, so like your father. He wanted the world to be run by wisdom and superior intellect, so very Aristotelian. And you, *mon cheri*, are like me. Do not bother to protest, my son who 'as a *penchant* for pool halls; you 'ave the suspicious nature. A tool of survival."

"Why, Ma? I trashed my junior year. I blew it because I thought I..."

"It can be repaired. I need to be dead for awhile until some issues become clear."

"Issues? You abandoned me because of ISSUES? You could have told us, me."

"You? Monsieur Blah Blah Mouth? The boy famous for ruining surprise birthday parties?"

"That's not fair! I was like eight or nine."

"You were eight *and* nine. The human *telegraphe*. And the retirement party for Mr. Post just two years ago. Never 'ave I understood your compulsion to tell to everyone all that you know." Joe wanted to tell her that he had decided on his own to fix that problem, but he wasn't telling her now for anything!

She continued, "Everyone 'ad to believe that I am dead, especially you. Especially our neighbors and your friends. I 'ave taken a tremendous risk coming to you, Joseph. There must be secrecy, *mon grand*. It is the oceans that are at risk." She signaled him to come to her. He shook his head. Her lips tightened. "Gilbert 'as charge of you. You may go."

Joe went to the door and paused, and then kept walking without looking back. He had refused her Old Country Catholic Blessing—the sign of the Cross on his forehead which she then kissed. His cool, understandingly dad would have smacked him into the next county.

When his brain settled to where he could walk in a straight line despite the anger, the lightning bolts, and the surges of doubt, he entered the crisis center. The Gorilla Glass was plastered with headlines. Joe read a few:

*Dentists east of Vancouver refusing patients

*Tribal hatcheries of the Colville Tribes in Washington State attacked by a pack of Reanimates. The governors of California, Washington and Oregon call in National Guard

*Many towns order stat cremations

*Some accidental murders cite Fish Head Fever. Man shoots neighbor, claiming he was "fish-head crazy". Under arrest for lack of evidence of fever and a history of multiple confrontations

*Increased sales of hockey masks

*Fishmongers cutting off fish heads and putting them out back of the store

*National Guard closes the beaches. States of emergency. Civil rights protests

*Fish Head Roulette parties on some campuses

A family of three recovers from Fish Head Fever

The beautiful doctor was addressing the seamen. "...so that is what I can tell you about pineal glands: they produce melatonin, nothing more. The same melatonin which is available at the drug store. The lab samples of urine and blood and spinal fluids are being sent to the lab in Santa Barbara. Our doctora will test them there. She expects to get there in two days—most likely ahead of the samples. She will also test for a corticotrophin-releasing hormone excreted by the hypothalamus which controls the body's response to physical and emotional stress and is responsible for stimulating anxiety.

"Personally, I wonder if we have a neurotoxin at work." Melusine noticed Joe. "You will work from your computer in the sickbay lab, Joseph. Do not enter this space until you are cleared. Please concentrate on new incidences and map them." She continued talking then to the small room packed with seamen in dark blue uniforms. "Seaman Oliver, any data from Missing Persons?"

But wait! Mommy said I can be out of my room. Joe trudged down to midship. *Mommy ain't gonna do nothin' for me now.* As he approached the sickbay/lab area, he saw a guard with a semi-automatic gun, full-size, not a sneaky one like Gil sported. The guard took a step back. *Whoa. He's afraid of me! Like I'm gonna turn him into a Zombie!*

"State your business."

"Doc told me to work on the sickbay computer." His answer was a quick nod. Joe sat at the lab desk...and looked at Dario still strapped onto the litter. The pulse ox was on an earlobe, an electroencephalogram probe was taped to his forehead. Technically, he was dead. No pulse on the readout, but a steady stream of brain *stuff* spit out on the EEG machine. It looked random, but there it was.

Dead? Not dead?

Joe wondered if they would feed him fish brains if he woke up. And why didn't he look all bloodless? And when would Gil take his head off? Joe thought of the clinical ice queen running the crisis center above, hungry for data. "Sorry, dude," he whispered. "You're research...me, too."

His eyes caught the gleam of metal next to his computer. A coil of thin cable with metal handles on either end lay near the mouse pad of the old screen. A Gigli saw. His granddad used one to take small branches off his fruit trees. Joe nodded. "No worries, dude. Gil's on it."

He logged in and went to the spread sheet. Maya Chen...died at 1251. And reanimated at 1451. Two hours exactly.

Joe picked up a clipboard and read. "State of California, Department of Health Services, Full Name, Place of Death..." Dario was 27. "Immediate Cause of Death: Septicemia...Other Conditions: Fever of Unknown Origin."

The CTB was 1805(PM). *That's when he died. Those bells were for him.* Something caught his eye and Joe used the telecam to check out a small red boat turning toward open water. A rigid-hulled inflatable with an inboard motor water jet. Two passengers and the one steering had a thick ponytail.

The computer clock said 1835. *An hour-thirty to go...*

Joe's research hadn't reached beyond the West coast. He typed in Washington State. *Good ole Seattle had seven primary cases. Spokane? Ten! Hmmm.*

By 1900 hours, Gil was sitting next to him in full Hazmat, elbows on desk, chin resting on steepled, gloved hands. "The Director was never here."

"In so many ways," said Joe. He had better things to think about than his mother, like the State Police reports of Washington, Oregon, Montana, Idaho, Wyoming and Nevada. There were dozens of cases of FHF—with home-grown zombies crawling out of the deserts and down the hillsides. But the odd thing—beside zombies—was that they weren't from any particular place. They were from west of Ely, north of Lolo, south of Fish Creek, places that were specks to begin with. Seen from Google Earth, most were just a few farms and a road.

Gil tensed. He punched in a number on the phone. "Mellie, get down here."

Joe looked at Dario—did he just move? Like a twitch? "He's kicking the bag!"

The EEG now showed spikes and valleys. Doc B strode in and stared through the window and back at the readouts. Gil shook his head. He picked up the Gigli saw.

"No," she said.

"When is when? That poor boy isn't going to lie there forever just to satisfy your curiosity."

"I am not ready, Gilbert. No. This is the only chance any of us *anywhere* will have to observe the natural course of this disease! End it now, and you put us weeks, *months,* behind."

"It's not right," he yelled, nose to nose.

"None of this is right," she yelled back, "but Luz Marina loses her son and nothing is gained? Nothing that will help? Gil...she knows. Oh, she knows. That why she left."

"Um, "said Joe, pointing. "The bottom of the bag." The bottom of the body bag had expanded, stretched, filled. And now it was moving up and down.

Melusine sat between them. Gil looked at her and picked up the phone. "Red, what is the status on the beach bum from Night One? Not found? Still not found?" He hung up and raised his eyebrows at the doctor. "You want data? Put Dario underwater and see who takes a bite, because this might be the really big problem."

Chapter ten

Melusine's jaw dropped. "I never thought of that..." Now, she looked stricken. "The contagion could reach the oceans! Oh my, oh my..."

Gil held his chin with his hand, staring at the body bag. "That's a tail. I didn't know the boy had swim capacity."

"He did," said Melusine. "He preferred feet."

Joe had other questions. "Are you going to feed him fish heads?"

"No," she said.

"So we're going to like starve a zombie?" Joe frowned. "It just doesn't sound right."

"This is not *World War Z*, Joe. Dario has nerve firings in his brain. That's what we know from the EEG. I think it is a neurotoxin."

"I read that book," said Gil. "The author walked around with a shotgun. So what *do* we know, Melusine?"

She shook her head. "Nothing. Not one conclusive, incontestable fact. Fish, fish heads, sea food, food. None of it is causative. Some live, some die, some die and reanimate. I am hoping the chromo spectrometry on urine samples will show something. Anything of interest, young Joe?"

"Yeah, the outbreak is being reported way out in the Rockies."

"Can you pursue? Ask about diets?"

"It's from State Police read-outs. You'll have to get me get started, sir," Joe said, looking at Gil.

Gil sat. "I'll talk to them. So back to our boy here. What are we waiting for?"

"Well, Gilbert, he has not really 'awakened' yet. I want to evaluate that. We're coming up on the two-hour mark. There are some ion-channel neurotoxins, polypeptides that promote spontaneous and repetitive neuronal firing." Gil and Joe stared. "Think poisons!" she said. "There are 18 million spider venom proteins—we're just talking spiders here! One of them, dortoxin, can cause convulsions and tremors and hyperactivity up to thirty seconds AFTER death."

"You want like a new toxin?"

"Yes." She nodded. "I want to find a new toxin. People can now make proteins in their kitchens. There are molecular 3D printers—God save us all! Pandora and her zillion boxes." She propped her chin in her hands on the desk. Joe noticed how tired she looked. "A synthesized protein, then, or an unknown one from nature. Our Dario has to be patient. Most cities are cremating bodies immediately after death. We are lucky to have him."

"Oh, for God's sake, Mellie! Let him go."

"Especially after you say the oceans are at risk. He might hold the key, Gilbert. Anyway..." She put her head down on the desk. "Let me rest for a few minutes."

As Joe studied the long lashes resting on dark circles below her eyes, Gil slid and tapped his finger on his phone. "Bill? How the deuce are you, you ole cowpoke? The family? Good. No, I'll be up in June when the pass opens. Can't wait to ride the fences. Hey, I'm still sailing with the Coast Guard and we're right in the middle of this Fish Head Fever crap. Yep, I know. One of my men picked up on that. I'd like him to be able to call the families of these folks and ask about their diets. Our chief doc thinks that's the key...nope," Gil shook his head, "not one single fish to connect them. That was last week's thought... Boopdiddly, indeed...ah, let me write that down. Thanks, Bill. Looking forward to some rodeos. Great. Yeah." Gil hung up and pushed the paper to Joe. "Use this code to get into the data base. You can use his name. Coronel William Washington. Advisor to the Chief Executive."

"The President?!"

Gil shook his head. "Governor."

Joe got into Montana's Highway Patrol system and starting making data pages with names and phone numbers. He didn't want to be on the phone talking diets when Dario "woke up". Done, he hit 'Save'. "How old is Luz Marina?"

"Older than she looks." Gil stared ahead.

"Fifty?"

Gil made a face judging the statement. "Good guess."

"You're not going to tell me, are you? I thought since we're all in this stupid HLA tribe, you'd let me in on some stuff."

"I'll let your mother."

"What's a Director."

"Same answer."

Gil and Joe sat cross-armed staring at Dario with Melusine asleep between them.

Joe was almost asleep when dreadful growls started coming from Dario's throat. His jaw worked, open close, open close. His eyes opened and he turned his head left and right. "Right on time," said Joe. "He sees us."

"Maybe," said Gil. "Mellie, wake up, girl."

The three watched Dario buck the restrains. "Will they hold?" she asked.

"They will," said Gil. "They can hold five hundred pounds in a gale."

Melusine waved her arms above her head. That elicited louder growls. "Now, sit still." After a few minutes, the reanimated seaman straightened his head toward the ceiling and continued fighting the restraints. Gil stood and reached for the hazmat suit. "Gil, no!"

"Are you going to put him in the water?"

"Do we have a shark cage?" she countered.

"Too late for that."

Melusine sighed and shook her head.

"Then," said Gil suiting up, "I'm going in." Melusine made to protest. Gil shook his head. "I love this boy. I watched him grow up. Alive, dead, I don't know. But I do know that he's suffering and this is wrong. Get your needles and bottles ready, girlie, 'cause it's over."

Melusine sat very straight. "I know how it must be to lose a—"

"You DON'T know."

Joe didn't know where to look. At Melusine, abashed but still stubborn. Or Gil, whose face was screaming pain and rage. Joe studied the keyboard.

"Suit up, boy," Gil said, curling his fingers around the Gigli saw. "I'll need a hand."

"Wait!" said Melusine. "Face covers!"

Joe stepped into and zipped up a hazmat suit and adjusted the plastic face protector. *Whoa, here's one for the college application.* Without a shred of embarrassment, Joe hid behind Gil as they went into the sickbay, glad for the guard with the rifle at the door.

"Get behind him. Stay out of reach of his fingers and, need I mention, his mouth. I need you to keep his head absolutely still. Now, let me get under him." Gil sat on the floor with his legs extended beneath the stretcher and his butt below Dario's head. He stretched to put the wire cable on Dario's throat. "Don't watch."

Joe didn't. But he heard the late Dario's growls turn into hisses as Gil's arms pulled in alternate rhythm through the cartilage of his throat. He heard the wire shh, shh through the bones of the spine. He heard himself gag. He felt the head disconnect and lay held in place by the block of memory foam.

"Son—" Gil looked him in the eye. "Well done. Tell the doc to come in."

Joe felt so awkward being in the middle of their battle. Melusine stood there waiting; she didn't need to be told anything. He waved her in anyway with flipper hands, feeling like some idiot sea lion. All in hazmat herself, and carrying a tray packed with syringes and vials and bottles, she sidled past him at the door.

"Joe, can you help me?" She spoke looking at Gil. "The commander needs to make arrangements with the captain for the cremation." Gil stood silently, then left.

"Are we sure he's all dead?"

"Young Joe, I know nothing for sure. And I cannot tell you how profoundly that bothers me...but the EEG is flat and his spine is irreparably severed. While I set up, would you unzip the bag without undoing the straps?" Joe worked slowly, not catching his gloves in the zipper teeth. "Take the scissors and cut the shirt and pants open, just to the top of the pubis." Joe cut the shirt. He lifted the waistband of the sweatpants, silently apologizing to Dario. *"Pubis, huh?"* He stopped at three inches below his belly button.

"Good." She collected every body fluid Joe could image from his head and mouth and spine and brain.

"He looks dead now."

"What do you mean?" she said.

Joe said, "I saw this dead dude on the beach once. The top of him was white like a fish belly, and the bottom half, the half on the sand, looked like he was full of grape jelly."

"Ah, lividity. The blood had congealed. With Dario, whatever made the blood circulate has stopped. Or whatever gave him that high color has changed. We may know soon." She unlatched the strap around his forehead. "Help me now. Do not let his head drop." Together, they eased the body bag over his head and pulled the two-way zipper down to his chest. Joe made to replace the ratchet strap on his forehead and then stopped...what did he expect from a severed head?

"You do not have to watch." Melusine held a scalpel over his abdomen. "I could not ask Gil to do this."

Joe thought he could watch; he'd watched "Bones" and "NCIS" since he could walk. And his father had long dissected seals, sharks and other creatures in front of him. But when she began to cut through the skin and the fat and the fascia, Joe had to look away. This was a human being, not special effects, a man he'd bunked with, a man who was fun and kind-hearted and who loved his mother.

She took stuff from his lungs and liver and stomach and parts he didn't know. "Oh dear, someone's turning green. Open the scuttle." Joe put his nose out the round window at the welcomed horizon and took deep breaths. "One more, darling."

Huh?

Joe looked over at her; she was speaking softly to Dario as she attached a wicked long needle to a 20cc syringe. Deftly, she inserted it into his bladder and withdrew whatever urine there was. "I loved you, too."

#

Joe went to his berth for a moment of privacy. He'd just learn a whole lot about two fellow merms aka swimmers. Gil had a ranch in Montana and had lost a kid, and Doc B should be called Mellie, Princess Warrior. *She protects her own, even Ole Crusty ...and then there's Ma, protecting the whole stupid ocean. Life beyond West Seattle High.* Joe felt like a whiney little kid thinking he was something—

He looked at his bunk. "Whoa, my clothes!" The Eighties dude must have dropped off the Target bag before heading to the hills. "What if *he's* one of the zombies crawling down the Big Horn? Or his old lady?" he thought. "We need some Zombie drones!"

#

"You look dapper," said Melusine, later. Joe nodded, feeling better in cargo shorts and long tee. "I do not know," she continued, as they both looked across Monterey Bay from the deck, "about the tail fin. Depends on where we send him."

"Suits me," Joe said, having no idea what she meant. "I'd like to go on shore. You'll tell Gil?"

"Tell me what?" The commander stepped next to him on the deck.

Joe frowned. Gil was more warden than babysitter. "I want to go on shore."

"Go. We're doing the red eye to Santa Barbara." Loose strands of long hair shifting in the breeze, Gil pointed a long finger close to Joe's nose. "That is the first piece of classified information I've given you. Don't blow it."

Joe turned to go.

"Son!" Joe stopped, bracing for whatever orders Gil had to give. "Here's a twenty."

Joe stood still. Did he look like that little boy, then, the whiney one inside still complaining about high school crap? "Thanks, sir, but I'd like to earn that."

"You did."

Melusine nodded. Joe took the money, gave a silly, snappy salute and bounded down the brow.

Dude, it's sweet to be on land. He headed to a patch of green beyond the vast Coast Guard parking lot, crossing the street to where there was a kayak store. Out front was a vendor's box for *The Enquirer. "BIGFOOT HAS FISHHEAD FEVER!"*

That sorta like makes sense. Come on, Agent K." As he scanned the gossip headlines, the air around him changed. Joe felt edgy, nervous.

"Hey, kid!" A dude in a black-and-gold Steelers shirt ten feet away held up his hand to his eyes. As he lowered it, the hand curled into a gun and he pulled the pretend trigger. Smiling, he walked away.

Suddenly, Joe didn't want to be on land in a city he didn't know. He walked quickly up the brow and stood at the door to the crisis center. It was as much home as any other place on the planet. And Gil was now calling him 'son', not 'boy'.

"Who was the clown with the sunglasses?" Joe turned and stared at Gil. "Come into my office." He followed him to a tiny space crammed with phones and computers.

"You saw him?" said Joe. "How?"

"CCTV from the parking lot. He threatened you?"

"Yeah, made like he was going to shoot me. I don't know who he is. I saw someone like him before, in Seattle."

"You have my full attention."

"Well, like, there's this arcade, Brufsky's, not in the nicest part of town."

"Your mother wouldn't approve." Gil's eyebrows lifted.

"Dad knew. I've been going there since I was twelve, when school got boring. They have some pool tables in the back and let me play for pizza...you don't have to look so judgmental!"

"Didn't say a word," Gil said, studying him over steepled fingers.

"There's this black dude who comes in, never plays, just sits. Has a beer."

"Looks like...?" Now the steepled fingers were tapping.

Joe paused, trying to remember accurately. "Lean, average height. Long dreads. Always wears a black shirt—either with a yellow tie or a gold vest with thin black stripes. And those shiny military shoes."

"Patent leather?" Gil said, incredulously.

"Yeah, and he limps."

"And this guy?"

"Wait. He also has yellow aviator glasses."

"Shooting glasses," Gil said, mostly to himself.

"So *this* dude has an Asian face and a ninja pony bun. And a really sick amber visor, kinda Star Trek."

"Care to continue in English?"

"Had a Pittsburgh Steelers jersey on...Black and Gold?" Joe figured the old guy needed some elucidation. "And he had shiny gold high tops. And," he said, anticipating Gil's question, "a limp."

Gil rubbed his lip. "Might be a total coincidence."

"Maybe it's a gang with a weird dress code."

"I am looking into it. Any names you can remember?"

"They called the black dude T-Cat. One guy calls him Tez."

"Taz?"

"Tez. This dude pointed his finger at me like it gun and pulled the trigger," Joe shook his head. "Creeped me out! I couldn't have done anything to him. I never saw him before...whoa. At Target! He was right behind me in line and I grabbed the National Enquirer and he was kinda looking at it...maybe I super annoyed him. But to follow me...?"

"Stay onboard. Get some chow. Cook's outdone himself tonight with fresh Institutional Hamster."

Joe refused to ask.

Gil gave a tiny smile.

Chapter eleven

Joe was cutting into a "hamster" when the seaman Gil called Red sat down with a loaded tray. "How ya doin', little buddy?"

"Is this supposed to be Chicken Cordon Blue?"

"Shh, you'll hurt Cook's feelings and then I'm outta luck. I do like my chow. Man, I miss Dario. He was my Chow Club buddy."

"Like huh?"

"Dario was lean and mean. So Capt'n had him lead PT for me and Hullmaster Slick—"mandatory physical activity" for us ample-proportioned guys."

Joe tried to extract the cheese and ham from the chicken. "How long did you enlist for?"

"We enlist for eight years, the first four are active. Gotta do something with my time...besides eat. What's next for you, buddy?"

Joe almost started to tell him, but remembered the "blah blah mouth" comment from his loving mother. He shrugged, instead. "Need-to-know basis, I guess."

"Got that right!" said Red, who had somehow eaten one chicken breast rolled with cheese and ham while talking to him, and was starting on the second.

#

It was after midnight when the boat docked at Santa Barbara. Gil found Joe in the mess watching ESPN. "We're going for a ride."

"Are you shipping me out somewhere?" Joe didn't know if he should be worried, but he was.

"No."

"It's dark."

"Yes, Nancy. That's why were debarking now."

They drove an unmarked military vehicle up to a old large house. "Where are we?" said Joe.

"Your mother's. Not a word."

"Not a word? Oh, I got plenty of words on this one. She let me think she was dead. She abandoned me. What kind of mother does that?!"

"Sometimes people don't have a choice."

"I don't buy it."

"I don't care." Joe didn't move. Gil looked at him. "When you're ready to man up, Nancy, come in the house."

Joe decided he did not want to sleep in the car and in his mind's eye Dominic Comstock was raising a stern eyebrow. *I'll tell her she's a terrible parent later; at least I'll have the element of surprise.* She was standing at the stove in a Mexican-style kitchen, the walls and counter covered with blue-on-white tiles. It looked authentic, old.

"'Allo, *mon grand.*" She handed him a mug of steaming hot chocolate. "It's the real stuff," she said. "And sit, I don't want it on the floor. Any news, Gil?"

"Well, Annie, Mellie's not got a single conclusive thing. She's banking on Dario's autopsy results."

She crossed herself. "Poor baby."

Joe studied this new mother called "Annie". Her hair was shorter and boyish. She stood barefoot in a swooshing black and gray caftan and was even wearing silver earrings and a row of skinny bracelets. She looked sophisticated, *tres* French...not the mother from the PTA meetings at West Seattle High who had unfailingly worn white deck sneakers, jeans skirts, jeans jacket and blue striped tee-shirts—the mime uniform, Martin called it. Only on Sundays did she change to a black dress and bright sweater.

Anne-Sirène turned to her son. "Joseph, I 'ave planned for you to visit Westmont College tomorrow. There is a tour for prospective students at 1 PM. And the day after, you can check out the University of Santa Barbara."

Same crap, different house! "Ma, I dropped out."

She raised an eyebrow. "Technically, you did not. Life does not end at fifteen; nor have you made your quota of mistakes."

"Thanks, Ma." *I'm so confused.*

"Gil, I trust you are enjoying the company of my youngest son."

"I've had worse details."

"Excellent. Joseph, let me show you to your room."

Joe drained the mug and followed this different woman in her flowing silk through to a small bedroom. "I liked you better in Seattle."

"*Mai, oui.* I am *tres* kind to the young and the weak," she said. "It is to be 'oped you will strengthen and grow." A kiss on the cheek and she was gone. In short order, Joe was lying in a real bed thinking about his new mother—a woman who could cut you off at the knees in a heartbeat. "Not enough data," his father would say, and he fell asleep.

In the morning, Joe explored his mother's secret house, starting at the front door. He felt like he was in an old Spanish mission, except it was too fancy. White walls, timber ceilings inside. Stucco and really ornate stone trim and old-time iron work, outside. Soon, his mother was at his side, with her usual steaming coffee. "What is this place, Ma?"

"It was built by your grandfather of sorts in 'onor of his grandfather who said that 'is daughters should "kiss iron", and built a Spanish Revival."

"Huh?"

"The grille work. Spanish girls were kept very much apart from men, but they were allowed to speak through the iron bars."

"Did you? Kiss iron?"

"Papa was being silly." She sipped her coffee and sighed. "This was a fine *casa* in its day. Today, the land is worth more than the 'ouse. But such a fine view where I can keep the people I love in my 'eart."

They walked through tended gardens, a swimming pool and side privacy walls of old cypress trees and a view of the Pacific that stretched unbroken.

"What are those?" Joe pointed to dark lumps on the horizon.

"The Santa Barbara Channel Islands. People visit them by ferry, if you're interested."

"Ma, why aren't you hiding? I thought you were on the lam."

"Finn—you will meet him—'as sufficient anti-drone equipment up for me to be out of doors for a moment, but you're right. I do miss my front balconies." They went in and settled in a sunny breakfast nook. None of this furniture was bought at Walmart, thought Joe.

"Ma, are you rich?"

Her delicate features compressed a bit as she thought. "I control many resources. Perhaps seeing me as a steward of wealth is more fitting. Why?"

"We could have had more vacations."

She laughed. "We went to New York, Paris and New Orleans. And when we did go, you boys—especially you—were cemented to the cable TV in the 'otel."

"We were deprived at home!"

"So deprived."

"Did Dad know?"

She nodded, smiling. "We 'ad an arrangement: he would pay for everything—and I was free to work if I wanted—and I would pay for university or whatever training you boys wanted. Sending you off today is a way to 'onor that arrangement." She tapped his arm with one finger. "Are you angry at me, *mon fils?*"

"Yeah, some."

She nodded. "I can bear 'some'."

Joe felt a little ashamed. "Ma? Was it because I blab everything that you didn't tell me?" Unexpectedly, his throat tightened.

"That was a large part of it, Joseph. I also chose to protect you."

"Ma?"

"*Oui?*"

"Do you know where Dad is?"

"No, *mon cheri*. But I do not believe him dead—my 'eart does not believe he is dead. We have no evidence. But neither 'as anyone contacted us for ransom."

Joe frowned. "I still think somebody kidnapped him."

She smiled sadly. "It is what I believe, as well."

#

Joe went on the Westmont College tour as prescribed. After mom saying it was her way of honoring Dad...oh, well. Rachel would love it here, he thought. Sprawling Santa Barbara/Goleta sat on a narrow ledge with the ocean in front and the Santa Ynez mountains behind. "American's Riviera" read the tourist signs. She'd also love the earnest students at Westmont. Christian, service oriented. Joe just felt like a dumb whiner.

"Well, sports fans?" asked Gil as they drove back to his mother's.

"Not a solution for toilet fish."

"Oh?"

"No, the engineering department is on another planet. I don't know. They talked about nano-engineering and multivariable Calculus. Classical mechanics versus relativistic mechanics." Joe sighed. "I want to build a hut in the woods and call it done."

To Joe's astonishment, Gil chuckled. "I tried that once. Turned into a five thousand-acre ranch. Try UCSB tomorrow."

The University of California at Santa Barbara was as close to the water as it could be. A third of the campus was The Lagoon. Joe knew this courtesy of Google. He'd read the prerequisites and doubted he could get in this school, either. *You dumb cluck. You totally blew high school! You're not ready for anything.* With a heavy heart, he got in the car with Gil. "This is a waste of time, sir. They're not going to let me in."

"Too bad. You're going." Gil dropped him off the University Center at the top bend of the lagoon. "I'll be in the parking lot by the Events Center. I'm sure good grades are cool, but what a man needs is a fire in his belly."

"Easier said than done," he muttered.

On a grassy patch to his left, a bunch of guys were beating one another with wooden sticks and swords. "Beware the Zompocalypse!"

Joe shook his head—they had no idea.

He looked up the slight rise towards the University Center. Nice place to skate, he thought, looking at a few skaters gliding their boards gently through the pedestrian students. Perfect concrete. With little enthusiasm, Joe reported to a very cheerful and pretty student rep and waited for the crowd to gather. Soon the rep gathered her "peeps" and started the tour. Her voice was so ridiculously high that he zoned out as soon as they left the lobby. He spied a really decent Alien skateboard going by. *Seven ply. Nice concave.*

The air shifted and sword whackers got quiet. "Oh, crap," Joe whispered. He turned to see a rich version of TezCat walking towards them.

"Hey, Comstock! Gonna get ya!" this TezCat shouted, and began a zombie shuffle toward him. Joe couldn't say why the figure was terrifying and not stupid-looking, but all of the students stepped back, frightened.

A student skater yelled, "Freak!"

"Gonna get you, too," he yelled and laughed.

One of the fighters shouted, "Get him! Get the freak!" And, as a group, they went after him with their wood and plastic swords, like cartoon peasants against Dracula. The one nearest TezCat swung at his head. TezCat jutted his chin and the dude somersaulted backwards. Then, he waved his hand, making a few stagger feet backwards, while the rest of them flew back as though an explosion had pushed them through the air.

Joe stepped up to the owner of the Alien board who stood frozen. Joe said, "Dude, he's after *me*! Give me your board and run!"

Amazingly, he did, so Joe pushed along the smooth pavement with his right foot, increasing his stride, doubling his speed. Three set, right turn, five set. Full speed, Joe made for the parking lot where Gil said he'd be. He glanced back—no Tez. With a deep breath, Joe eased up and rode a waving glide. A sharp turn left should get him close to Gil. He pressed the tail, made the turn...and rich TezCat was in front of him, one foot on a skateboard!

Joe almost bailed trying to avoid a collision. He began pushing, going as fast as he could...and alongside of him, skating goofy foot, was TezCat. Dang, he was smooth! Joe got wobbly and had to look away from the smug, sleepy expression.

"Joe, over here!" Gil stood beside the car with the engine running.

Almost there! Joe neatly dropped a final set when TezCat popped a massive Ollie and board-slid a perfect grind on the handrail. He bolted his landing in front of Joe while Joe fell hard on the concrete. TezCat stood over him with a smirk on his face.

Fear filled him as the stranger leaned over and slowly blew smoke in his face. "You're mine."

Joe coughed as Gil's Thunder Gut rumble reverberated down through his bones. His muscles responded; he crab-crawled till he could stand and sprinted towards the car. Slamming the door as Gil circled toward the exit, the strange man shook a no-no finger at them—still smirking—and walked away. Joe felt sick from the smoke and trembled.

Back in the house, Gil pushed Joe into a chair. "Annie, get in here!"

"What's wrong? Joseph?"

"We're calling your mother."

She struck a pose that screamed "I beg your pardon" and said, "What *catastrophe*

necessitates that?" Looking between the both of them, she settled into a chair and waited.

"You start," Gil said to Joe.

"I saw that guy again, the TezCat dude. He looked like a rich narco this time—long black ponytail, expensive black clothes. Big shiny gold medallion." He paused. "And gold-mirrored shades."

"Similar to the other actors," said Gil.

Joe resumed. "He starts zombie walking toward me, says "I'm gonna get you, Comstock" and he goes through this bunch of dudes doing stupid anti-zombie sword fighting and he just flicks them out of the way like "ping", you know, like he's flicking dead flies."

Gil leaned in. "What happens when he flicks them?"

"The dudes fly."

"They fall over?"

"No, they *fly*, like ten feet back."

"A tai chi master?" asked Anne-Sirène. Gil shrugged.

"He knew his way around a skateboard."

"Now he's on a skateboard? I'm confused," she said.

Joe continued. "This skate dude was freaking, so he gives me his board so I can escape and I'm zipping like crazy—you know I'm fast—jumping steps, and I turn a corner and creepy dude's there...with a board! I can see Gil and I'm like a hundred feet to go when Creepo TezCat ollies on the rail and 50-50s perfectly. And stomps the landing! It was so random, Ma!"

"How so?" said Gil.

"I couldn't have popped that high without some sort of kicker. There was no way for him to get up to that rail. I don't know how he did it...just crazy."

His mother said, "A tai chi master on a skateboard?"

Gil looked at her solemnly. "He laughed at my rumble."

Anne-Sirène frowned. "Hm, unexpected. I acknowledge we 'ave a problem. But why are we disturbing my mother for this? It seems that this character is just "messing" with Joe. That's the expression, *n'est-ce pas*?"

"He blew smoke in my face, Ma. And he said, "You're mine"."

Gil slowly shook his head. "He wasn't smoking, Annie. Any ideas? We're already missing one Comstock."

"Two, technically." Anne-Sirène stood and walked behind Joe. She wrapped her arms around him and kissed the top of his head. Then she tapped her Apple watch. "Finn will let us know when the secure WhatsApp is ready. Hot chocolate?"

Joe turned around to look at his mother. "I have another grandmother?"

She gave an exasperated look. "Let us say only "I 'ave a mother". I 'ave not inflicted her on any of my babies since the first one was born."

A tiny ping sounded on the Apple watch and Anne-Sirène pushed herself away from the tile counter. "*Allons-y.*" They followed her through a door, down three flights to a cave filled with electronic devices and screens.

"Looks like the Bat Cave," said Joe.

"The former wine cellar, now the lair of Finn." As she spoke, a lanky man with a lively face appeared. "Finn, this is my son, Joseph. Joseph, Finn Liban—he 'as a pool table."

"A gorgeous pool table," Finn corrected.

Anne-Sirène sat in front of the computer screen and sighed, "Let us get this over with." Finn nodded and she spoke, "Bon soir, Maman."

"'Evening, Grandmère," said Gil. "This session will be in English because of Joseph."

"And who is Joseph?"grumped a creaky voice.

Joe felt himself being pushed by Gil in front of the screen. "This is Joseph, Anne-Sirène's youngest son."

"Oh, for *pity's* sake! Are you still breeding?! No wonder the oceans are in such pitiful condition—"

"Yes, and 'allo again, Maman. We are sorry to bother you so late in the evening."

"So why *are* you are bothering me? Wait: Boy, let me look at you. Are you married?"

"No ma'am. I'm fifteen."

"That is no excuse and I am not "ma'am" to you, unless you feel particularly servile. You may call me Grandmère." She waited. Gil elbowed him.

"Thank you, Grandmère."

"Any sisters?"

"Huh? Ah, no...Grandmère."

"Just as well. Can't see that face on a girl. No daughters then, Anne-Sirène? Pity...Girl! You may cream my feet as we talk." Joe wriggled away and stood where he could see the screen, and hoped his mother's horrifying mother couldn't see him.

"We need to ask you about a disruptive character threatening my Joseph," said his mom.

"From here in Egypt?"

"Egypt? I thought you were in Albania."

Grandmère turned a sour face. "You have not kept up with your own mother."

"Do not dare to judge me, Maman. We are talking about California."

Grandmère shook her very wrinkled head. She had a more square face with higher bones than his mom, more like his own, really. After a long, imposed-upon sigh, she said, "Continue."

Gil continued. "A man of different appearances or a gang of men, has been confronting Joe by name. He—or they—always wear black clothes with gold in some form. A tie or vest or medallion. Always with some style of amber or gold sunglasses. Shiny shoes and a limp."

"No."

"Nothing? Ever? No ancient count or warrior?"

"No, Gilbert. Shaded-glass eyewear is so contemporary, just since the Twenties, really. I don't recall bronze or gold visors being wore except at investitures—although the gorget became incidental during all those revolutions. Does this man do anything of interest?"

Gil shook his head. "He seems to have excessive personal power beyond the laws of physics."

The old lady looked off into space.

"Maman?"

"Perhaps a man I should have liked to have known." One sigh and the dreamy look fell from her features. "Hmm...now, this sounds like an American character to me. Are you two not the American experts? I would think after a few centuries you should know enough. I put your ignorance down to the constant bearing of children, Ann Sirène. The company of whom slaughters the gray cells!"

The eponymous daughter asked, "Have you spoken with Zima lately?"

"Girl!" Joe watched Grandmère bop an ancient bent woman on the head with a flyswatter. "That webbing is tender. Keep it up and I'll have an infection!" She held the flyswatter like a scepter. "Yes, Zima and I had a lovely visit before she packed in for the winter."

Gil said, "Does she have a cell phone?"

Grandmère sighed. "Nephew, she is buried deep in the mud somewhere in Ukraine. If I am to have any peace, I see I must give you Bunya's phone number. Girl, my book."

Anne-Sirène whispered, "Two hundred years and she hasn't bothered to learn her name." Then she smiled and addressed the screen. "Maman, is there anything it you would like? Chocolates, *perfum*, clothes?"

Grandmère squinted towards the camera. "What about that which you are wearing? Stand up. I shall take one of those, but in gold."

"I shall try, Maman."

"And the peppermint bonbons."

"York peppermint patties? Certainly. And you, Thessa?"

"A Michael Bublé CD, if Madam pleases."

Moving the address book back and forth for focus, Grandmère spoke. "Here is the number. Finn, are you ready?"

"Jawohl, mein Emperess!"

Grandmère giggled. "Such a charmer, our Finn." She then read a line of 20 to 30 characters and numbers.

Finn strode to one of his terminals. "I'll have that for you in a minute, Anne-Sirène."

"If you're finished, we are getting ready to watch our *telenovela*—which one are we watching?"

"*Pasión y Poder*. Mexican!" the ancient servant added with a shy grin.

"And I want that special cream on both fins, girl. Oh, Alphonse wrote me at Christmas."

"*Alphonse* did?!"

Joe had never heard that tone of voice from his mother. She was thoroughly hurt and surprised.

"Yes, he is my spiritual confessor. Did you not know he is the priest of Saint Tadros of Shatby? He lives across the street."

"No, I didn't know," said Anne-Sirène. "Feel free to give him my address."

The "girl" gave a faint wave as her mistress hit the "end" button. The frame went black.

"Whoa," said Joe.

"Woe, indeed," said his mother.

Chapter twelve

"We're going back to the *Castro*," said Gil.

"Joe needs to eat. Sausage and Brie, my love, or a crepe with Nutella?"

"A crepe, please. And hot chocolate?" Joe felt better already. "Who is Alphonse?"

"My son...of my first family. Your 'alf-brother, I suppose. I believed 'im dead."

As she worked her magic at the stove, she said, "Any progress, Gil? Anything from InterPol?"

"InterPol has reports that match the costume, but no real crimes. Just 'Persons of Interest'. Although, things always happen when these sorts are around: buildings burn, factories explode. But never any proof. And there's a kiddy cartoon with TezCat as a character."

"*Vraiment*?"

"It wasn't a cartoon," said Joe, "it was a Nintendo game: Inazuma Eleven."

Gil continued. "It's sporadic. There is mention of similar persons of interest in the Cold War and before World War One. He was in Sarajevo the day Archduke Franz Ferdinand was assassinated."

"White dude?" asked Joe.

"'Caucasian' was mentioned once. And the pre-World War I man was 'swarthy'."

"Still I think it is a Tai Chi master, with or without a skateboard. I shall ask an associate from China," said Anne-Sirène, placing a neatly folded crepe and a mug of melted chocolate and cream before him.

Joe swallowed and sat very still. "Ma, I missed your cooking." She wrapped her arms around him and he inhaled. "It will all be fine," she said.

"Why did *your* mother—"

She stood, laughing. "You learn quickly."

"Yeah, so what's wrong with my face?" His mom gave him a blank look. "She said she couldn't see my face on a girl," Joe explained.

Hands on hips, she shook her head. "Ruslana Jelenaslava, Countessa of Herzegovina, 'as never in her most ancient life held an audience with her glasses on."

"She wanted your dress."

"She trusts my taste, and Thessa is not allowed on QVC. It would raise suspicion."

"Okay," said Joe, filling his fork with Nutella. He paused it midway to his mouth and turned to Gil. "How did you know?" he asked him. "You had the car running, ready to roll. Am I bugged? Did Melusine implant a chip?"

Gil raised his finger. "Your mother will tell you." He turned tired eyes to Anne-Sirène. "He asks too many questions, your boy."

"You are family," said Anne-Sirène. "He just knew."

"Whoa! I'm related to..., he fumbled, pointing to Gil. "That's gnarly."

Gil grimaced. "I hate that word."

"Are we cousins? I can call him 'Cuz'?" This was wild, thought Joe, a new horizon...

Gil folded his arms. "Nothing changes, Fuzznuts. No one will know that we are kin. No one. So no 'Cuz', no 'Uncle', nothing. No strings to the Director, do you understand?" Joe nodded. "No, you don't. Any connection of me to you puts *her* in danger, making *you* a liability...and a target."

"Okay, okay!"

"And," Gil continued, "if anyone asks about your private life, your family, your pets, your plans, your past, say nothing. And tell me."

"I can have amnesia from the storm...and the fever."

Anne-Sirène smiled at Gil and nodded toward Joe. "He's thinking. Overly dramatic, but thinking."

Gil shook his head and pointed at Joe. "Get your gear. I'm in the car. Till later, Annie...and answer his questions before he annoys the niceness out of me."

"So, ask, *mon grand*."

Joe started. "Did Dad know?"

"Please, *mon cheri*, complete sentences or it will make for a very long night."

"Did Dad know you were a mer, um, swimmer? When you married him?"

"Yes, he knew and he knew right away. I was not being as careful as I should 'ave been and he spied me with my tail out on Puget Sound. It was either marry him or be dissected." Joe started coughing. "I am joking, Joseph. *S'il vous plait!*"

"What part are you joking about?"

"I <u>was</u> swimming and he <u>did</u> see me and we 'ad "the thunderbolt" as we say in France. I was willing to be his wife."

"How old are you?"

"We 'swimmers' live very long lives. My family is exceptionally long-lived. You are not my first family, nor my first sons. But you are one of two surviving. My earlier sons fought duels and unerringly caught cannonballs. But, Alfonse, we now know, is a priest in Alexandria. They must think him very 'oly for his ridiculous age."

"Whoa," muttered Joe.

"Indeed," said his mother. "But no daughters. All my 'usbands thought that for the best. They thought I would be too severe with them. But is it not a grave responsibility to raise a daughter, a useful one? It is we who 'old civilization together." She brought the *chocolat* pot from the stove. "More?"

Joe nodded. One did not sneer at melted dark chocolate whipped with heavy cream. A thought popped into his head. "Ma, what does your name mean?"

"Anne-Sirène? Anne, mother of the Virgin, no ? And Sirène is French for mermaid. You did not know ?" She studied her son's face and shook her head.

"Your father named the sloop after me."

She continued, "And usually Coast Guard Cutters are named after Coast Guard heroes, but since ours concerns Monterey Bay, she was named her after an old friend, María Antonia Castro. We were dear friends, wives of the earliest landowners of Monterey Bay. The mission of Santa Barbara was later. My next 'usband, or so, purchased the land from Mr. Den who bought the old Mission.

"We threw many fine dinners and fiestas, María and I. And the Raphael Gonzales Adobe in the 'istoric neighbohood? Another collection of ghosts. You may see my wedding certificate to Garcilaso Hernández etcetera, etcetera, on the wall in my bedroom. It was not my first marriage either, Joseph, but the first in the New World."

"How many times have you been married?"

"Hmm. I need to count. Some were very short—long before antibiotics—but a marriage can be no longer than fifty, sixty years. I so enjoy being a wife...and mother."

Joe sat blinking.

"Enough for now?" she said. "I 'ave loved all of my children, Joseph. May I?" This time, Joe lowered his head and accepted her blessing. "Few of my children are swimmers, but a few lived long lives...and were mostly people of good reputation. You may start your life afresh in Santa Barbara, preparing for your calling...which may not be fixing the plumbing on an empty island. Look up Sisqouc School. It's a boarding school in Santa Barbara County."

Joe gave her a disgusted look.

"I'm dead, remember?" She raised an eyebrow in return. "Mr. Miller can 'elp you matriculate. You *'ave* spoken with him, no? *Mon Dieu*, Joseph."

"I've been busy looking for Dad." That took the wind out of her. "Mr. Miller left a few messages, said he was paying the credit card from the account."

"*Bon*," said his mother. "Your father will not appreciate 'is credit rating being trashed while 'e is...gone. Please thank Attorney Miller and ask 'im to continue." She gave him a quick hug and walked with him to the car.

He tossed his bag in the back and turned. "How old is Luz Marina?"

"A mere baby. When she is not so busy, you should ask her about her work."

"How about Melusine?"

"She's older," his mother smiled coyly. "Both would consider you still in diapers."

Joe rolled his eyes and tucked into the car. "Be safe, Ma."

By the time they turned onto the street, he realized she had not told him her age.

Chapter thirteen

A box holding a jacket was next to his bunk when he awoke; the tiny card at the bottom said "Maman". He took a deep breath, remembering the quick historical search he had made last night of Monterey Bay: the first Mass was held in 1771! His mother was at least 350 years old—probably closer to 400!

But the main thing was that she was alive. Joe stood taller as the wound of being alone began to close.

He strode to the galley, stuffed in some pancakes and happily listened to Captain Bannerman deriding the dregs of dreadful coffee in his cup. *Maybe the Commander—the one I couldn't possibly be related to—could hook me up with some guys for an afternoon land run.* Weirdly, somehow, Joe had landed on his feet.

"Hey Captain, how do I get my GED?"

"I'm not sure, kid."

Joe scowled. "You were sure last week."

"Before..." The Captain hitched his thumb over his shoulder. "Before..." He kept swinging his thumb.

Joe got it. "Before my mother..."

"Quick study, Comstock, quick study."

"So what am I supposed to do?"

The captain leaned in. "You're supposed to go to that boarding school in Sisquoc. Have you looked in to it?"

"Yeah, last night," said Joe. "I'm not going there."

"Based on?"

"Based on it's for losers whose parents screwed up."

"It's a highly regarded private school."

"Bunch of trust-fund sissies," said Joe. "Why else would you spend a lot of money to have your kids feed horses? They are spoiled, useless, and don't know shi—sorry, sir. It's their parents' last chance to make them normal. I think I'd last five minutes there before I punched one of them out."

The captain considered his statement and nodded. "Unbiased prejudice aside, what's *your* choice?"

"Bishop what's-his-name. Dad went to a Catholic high school. May I see your iPad? Here it is: Bishop Garcia Diego High School."

The captain stretched and pulled the image with his fingers. "And where are you going to live? Santa Barbara is pricey."

Joe pointed to the map. "See that? There's a trailer park right next to the place...or my mom's house."

Captain Bannerman shrugged. "See if you have a legal guardian, kid. Start there."

Joe found his desk in the crisis center, his by virtue of a genuine name tag! He took his second deep 'I-belong' breath of the day.

On his email server there was one new message from attorney Miller. *I am relieved to know you are alive, Joseph. The police have inquired of me, and, as you are a minor, I am obliged to tell them. Shall I give them an address? You may give me such; I shall treat it as privileged information.*

Joe responded: *I'm bunking on a Coast Guard cutter. I want to start high school in Santa Barbara this fall. Do I have a legal guardian? Oh, and Dad's credit card might be floating around the Pacific. It was on board the* Sea Wren *when she went down. Please keep paying it off.*

He was studying Rachel's Facebook page when Doc B passed behind him.

"Friend of yours?"

"Used to be."

Used to be before Martin died. No, that's not fair, he thought. She'd been awesome. When Mom disappeared she'd call and even talked to him at school. Half his friends dropped him when his brother died, the rest backed away with Mom's "death". He couldn't blame them. He might be cursed or something. Anyway, Joe became invisible and avoided...even newly "divorced" kids had their own lunch table.

He might have stayed in school until the spider posters went up. Nasty monster spiders with his face and "Black Widow Joe" written below were plastered on the hall lockers. Joe found out who posted them via a tip from the janitor. Punching out the jerk landed Joe time in detention *and* time with the guidance counselor *and* time with the grief counselor *and* a fine visit with the school police captain.

Suspended!

Suspension suited him. He never went back.

Doc B tapped on her table; Joe closed out of Facebook. "Good morning, all. Doctora Cabrillo will be joining us in a moment with the first definitive piece of information we have. In the meantime, continue diet interviews, demographic shifts, and locating the Reanz."

"Ah, Doc," asked a seaman. "Can we call them 'zombies'?"

Melusine shook her head. "I prefer 'reanimates', a term our commander abbreviates to 'Reanz.'"

Joe wondered if she'd slept since Dario came into sickbay; she yawned and, as she took a sip of coffee, the door opened. Gil held the door for Luz Marina, scanning faces as she entered.

He's like a shield, thought Joe. Always alert.

"Commander, do you have time to wait for our doctora to speak or would you like to address the sea lion incident now?"

"Now, if I may." The veteran soldier stood at ease, arms behind, chin tucked and scowling as he began. "CCTV footage and witnesses confirm that a male Reanz lunged at a male sea lion who returned the favor, eviscerating the moron. Said moron then continued out to sea, guts trailing. This now highlights the very present danger of Reanz in our western coastal waters. Most municipalities are closing beaches until further notice. This decision will likely serve municipal pocketbooks more than the citizenry as there is no surveillance to pay for, nor are there mandates to raise protective fencing." He nodded to a questioning seaman.

"What about protecting marine life, sir?"

Gil nodded. "That is the question, ladies and gentlemen. I shall recon with the Trues' commander at 1300 hours today. We do not, repeat, do *not* want to have every harpoon-crazy clown with radar down there scrutinizing the kelp forests. Melusine?"

"Thank you, Commander. Doctora?"

Dario's mother stood before them in a crisp white lab coat. She was still half bald.

With quiet poise she began. "Good day to all of you. I did not swim today because I, too, fear the extra surveillance of our Monterey Bay. I have studied all the specimens from all the victims of the Fish Head Fever, the deads. But not those with a small fever or the deads not found, of course.

"The results are simple. First, no people without the HLA-B*84 gene—our 'Swimmer' gene—make the Fish Head Fever. Next, all the victims with one HLA-B*84 became sick and recovered. These people with only one expression of the gene do not know why, but they love the water. They navigate boats; they make to be fancy mermaids; they love the fish very much. In general," said Luz Marina, "these people get sick and recover."

At this point, Melusine interrupted. "We also allow that some of these victims may have died from exposure, starvation, animal attacks or secondary infections."

Luz Marina nodded in accord. "Finally, all the victims who made sick and died had *two* expressions for the 'Swimmer gene'. We—all of us on this boat—have two or three: If you make the gills, you have three...and the Trues have four. Questions?"

"You mean that if we get sick, we die?"

"Yes." Luz Marina nodded. "That is what I mean."

Her stunned audience was silent until one asked, "How about Joe? He recovered."

"Yes," she acknowledged. "Joseph is unique, *gracias a Dios*. I only can suspect a change in his epi-genetics, his RNA. But I cannot say that he has immunity, only that he recovered once."

Joe felt a tiny squeeze on his heart.

The corpsman spoke. "Is there any possibility of crafting a vaccine using Joe's antibodies?"

"I will, with permission of Joseph, take blood today." Joe had a flash of being held down by burly sailors if he refused. "The first studies of his blood were not clear for bacteria or virus. But, after four days, his body can now tell us. I hope to know more soon. More questions?"

"What about the Trues?"

"They are at great risk." She pointed to another raised hand.

"Have we ruled out anything?"

"You know," she paused, "that we made no connection to fish as the cause. So please to continue to ask the questions of the diet. We find neurotoxins in the bodies of the Reanz. They are unexpected. *Tal vez* the causative agent is new, a genetic creation. The immune system defends in a wide manner. That is the problem: by the time the body can make new weapons against this new agent, it is too late.

"*Gracias*, everyone." She held out her hand. "Joseph, we go?"

Burly sailors still in his head, Joe followed meekly. He sat near the blood collection tubes. "What does 'Luz Marina' mean?"

She neatly lined up needle and vials, cotton and alcohol. "Light of the Sea. And now..." When she finished, she held cotton to the wound. "Tape?" He shook his head. "It is good to be brave, no? I think you have more practice than I." Luz Marina took his hand. "Joseph, I am glad you survived. I do not wish you had died in the place of my Dario. That is primitive thinking and not for a scientist, no?"

Joe nodded with his throat thick and left her to his samples.

#

Back in the crisis center, the mood had changed. Everyone seemed more focused; now, the fight was personal. The corpsman had messaged everyone saying there seemed to be a trend of allergic responses in victims to shrimp, with none having shrimp in their systems.

I'm allergic, Joe thought. And four of his victims had a shrimp allergy. As he sent their data over, he realized Gil was standing next to him.

"Something wicked this way comes," he quoted.

"By the pricking of my thumbs," finished Joe. Gil looked impressed. Joe shook his head. "Martin's fault. Shakespeare, right?"

"Right. Listen, what do you have on the Rockies?"

"Red and I think it's a supply-line thing. Something shipped in. Here's the map."

"We don't think they are merely survivalists, sir," said Red. "Privacy geeks could be getting stuff shipped in from here. They could be private militia."

"How about some zombie drones, sir?"

The commander shoot him a look. "Got it covered, but good idea, Fuzznuts." He came around to look at the dots and markers on the maps of Idaho and Montana. His phone rang. "Hey, you old cattle rustler. We've heard tell of some people dead after being attacked. Anyone I know? Merle's boy? Terrible...no way! Took down a horse? A horse?! I'm listening...terrible shame. Call anytime. Bye."

All eyes went to Gil. "In Idaho, ten people have been killed in 'classic zombie style', brains extracted. Eighteen people grossly infected— but not necessarily dead—have been blasted or decapitated by, I guess, anxious neighbors. And many folks are sick, children included."

"And the horse?" said Joe.

"Two Reanz brought down a gelding and ate its brain. That is strength far beyond that of living men. They used their hands, you hear me? Bare hands!"

At noon mess, the corpsman came and sat with him. "Good work, Joe," he said. "Our combined shrimp findings total seven." He handed him a bottle. "Here, take these. They're a good multivitamin."

Two other sailors sat across from them. Chocolate black and fish-belly white, they were the burly guys Joe had in mind earlier. Any of their tattooed arms would equal his thigh. "Let me see your arm," said one. "Where's the Band-Aid?"

Joe glared with a "duh" stare. *What am I, five? Have any of <u>them</u> soloed a sloop down the coast?* Reason crept in. *I get it. I'm the Vaccine Boy. Well, watch this!* He faked a sneeze. Two sets of eyes worried the corpsman who pointed to the vitamin bottle. "He's covered."

Joe considered the possible variations on sneezing, but settled for info. "What does a True look like?" he said.

The African-American seaman answered. "Tail's mottled, skin's blue. Kinda transparent like glass noodles."

The white-American seaman shrugged. "Never seen one."

"They got webbing, you know, between their fingers and toes," added the first. "That's all I got."

"Are they 'red and yellow, black and white'?"

"Nah, all the same."

Joe stood. "I want some coffee." All three men responded together "It'll stunt your growth."

"Stop it!" He filled a cup anyway and headed towards the exit. As Joe left the mess he was aware of all eyes following him. *They're going to protect me to death.*

Back at his desk he checked his email from attorney Miller. Who's my guardian, he wondered. Grandpa? Uncle Ernie, the crazy trucker? That would be rad. Or Gil? The envelope please...

Mrs. Imogene Lauder.

Missus Lauder?! Stinky Missus Lauder?

Martin, you're not gonna believe this one... Joe tried to wrap his head around this. What were they thinking? Maybe it was Dad. Maybe it was just to get him through high school, so didn't really matter and she was next-door. Yeah, that had to be it.

What next? Did he need to contact the new high school for forms; did she have to sign for his transcripts? *Too much for me*, he decided, and sent his questions back to Attorney Miller.

Later that day, Joe was relaxing at the rail when a crewman he didn't even know came up to him, grumbling. "What's the matter with you? Get away from the rail."

"We're docked, dude. I'm not stupid!" This was getting annoying.

Another crewman chimed in. "Not stupid? You sail through the Mavericks in February and you're not stupid?!" The first one grumbled, "You're important to the crew, Joe."

"I didn't ask to be important."

Somehow they swelled up like giant balloon figures. "Man up," one said.

Joe stayed at the rail. "So how is letting you treat me like a baby manning up?"

"Grow. A. Pair."

Joe turned his back. *I was happier when they just gave me a name tag.*

Chapter fourteen

The next morning, Melusine addressed the entire crew in the mess, the news having spread. "Our doctora went back to her lab. I assume you have questions concerning our homozygous gene status and probable certain death."

Gil raised his eyebrows, but stood at ease and said nothing.

"I'd say you were right, ma'am. But I'm feeling a little bit more than that," said the corpsman, standing. "What I'm feeling is targeted." That provoked the crew to talk all at once. Melusine waited until the room quieted. "You are not alone in feeling targeted, Corpsman. That may indeed be true."

A woman petty officer said, "Has our genome been mapped?"

Melusine crossed her arms. "That is classified."

The woman continued, "The human genome was completed in 2004. Can you tell us nothing?"

Melusine sipped her coffee before answering. "Our concern is where to store that information. Merely having the information would confirm our existence."

"Well, someone must have mapped us," said the man next to her.

"George, I will not confirm what I cannot prove. If a genetic weapon has *not* been made against us, could we be a new intermediary in an unknown pathway?

"For example, there is a virus that takes over an ant's brain. It makes the ant climb to the top of blade of grass—a most dangerous place—and lock its mandible on the tip of the blade, thereby maximizing the possibility that a sheep will swallow the ant and that the next phase of the virus's life may continue in the sheep's stomach." She yawned. "Either we have been targeted to be extinguished as a population, or we are in the middle of an unknown lifecycle."

"So you're saying we *have* been targeted," repeated the corpsman, confused.

Melusine sighed. "Sadly, that might be." She yawned again. "Any ideas you may have as to who is targeting us, please see Commander Muirgen. And speaking of our commander, he's here to give us an update."

"Morning, troops. Yesterday I met with the Trues. There are two issues. First are sightings and encounters with Reanz. Three Trues have seen four separate Reanz, identified by clothing. By encounters I mean contact. One True was grabbed from behind and bitten in the neck. He died quickly from bleeding. A second Reanz bit another True. His course more or less followed the three-day course of Dario: fever, weakness, lack of coordination, violence and death.

"The second issue is the possibility of widespread cross-contamination of sea mammals." He paused. "Erratic behavior has been spotted in a seal."

"Orca food," said Captain Bannerman. "Great heavenly days! Zombie orcas...who knows about this, Gil?"

"We do. We are asking for undersea drones to do surveillance." He nodded to the captain. "Get us to Santa Barbara, Pete."

Into the shock and gloom, Dr Vidmorya spoke. "We still need that causative agent, people. Our corpsman Franklin has compiled seven cases of victims who had shrimp allergies. Each one had either hives, redness or some shortness of breath the day of the fish-head delirium or the day before. But—and this is the point—none of them had ingested shrimp! So, what form of shrimp protein entered their system and how? Call every family member back, not only of confirmed reanimates, but of all missing persons. We're getting closer. Thank you."

Throughout the morning, Joe spoke to eighteen family members of missing persons in the mountains of Washington and Idaho. No, they'd said, no shrimp. Frozen tilapia or salmon or canned tuna. He stretched; it was nearly lunchtime. Climbing over the knee-knocker at the hatch, he went aft. They were moving now at a moderate speed due South.

Ahead, the chief petty officer stood with Gil and pointed west. Joe looked and saw two smaller boats. He knew they were rescue boats, 25 feet long and used by the Coast Guard like squad cars. (Joe had watched all the episodes of "High Seas Cops"—buff Coast Guard guys chasing poachers, terrorists, illegal aliens and smugglers. Could this finally be some action on the *Ma Castro*? He walked over to butt in—what was the worst Gil could do?) "Ready for action, Commander."

"Always decks to be swabbed."

"No, really, what's going on?"

Gil looked sideways at the CPO and nodded. The chief said, "Those two RBs have sonar. If they see anything suspicious below, they will confirm with the Trues and harpoon from the deck. The bodies they'll tow to the *Castro*."

"What's the sonar range, Chief?" Joe saw Gil frown. "What? It's not classified. I can find it on Google."

The chief answered. "12,000 meters, give or take. Before you get on our fine commander's nerves, here's the plan: we go south, we circle the Channel Islands."

"Thank you, Chief."

"Do not encourage him. He knows far more than he should." A sound had Gil checking his smart phone. "Boop*did*ly! That does it. You bored, Fuzznuts?"

"Name's Joe. We're going on a rescue boat with harpoons?"

"Chief, order me up a RIB."

"We're eating *lunch* on a rescue boat?"

"We're going to Santa Barbara, pronto." Joe felt deflated. "Look, son. They don't need me right now, and they might be able to get along without you...or you can ask twenty more people their favorite brand of fish-sticks."

And Joe found himself in a Rigid Inflatable Boat, or more properly, a Rigid-Hulled Inflatable Boat. *This is incredible*! They were skimming the water, the boat propelled by an inboard water jet.

"How fast are we going?" Joe shouted. Gil pointed at the speedometer: 45 knots. Sailor Joe calculated multiplied that times 1.15...

Whoa, 80 miles an hour!

Within minutes, Gil had tucked the craft at the Coast Guard quay and an MP was dropping them off on a side street a few blocks in from the water. Gil rang a bell and a tall lanky woman greeted them on the third floor. "Well, hey, good lookin'. It's been a long time." Not young, she had long jet hair with white roots and really high cheek bones. They hugged like they had been friends for awhile.

"Mighty fine to see you, Cheyenne."

"Who's the kid?"

"Possible recruit."

Cheyenne shook her head. "Can't be too careful." Joe stared ahead while she scrutinized him and shook her head again. "I can't see you as a babysitter, Chief, but I'm not surprised you're here."

Gil shook his head. "You saw it?"

"Right there on Facebook, so we all know it's true." She pointed to an ancient computer monitor. Joe looked. On screen were two images: Gilbert Muirgen receiving his "Budweiser" aka SEAL Trident medal in 1972, and Gilbert Muirgen standing with the Secretary of the Navy, 2012. He looked exactly the same. After forty years, not a wrinkle. The headline asked, "Muirgen the immortal?"

They walked through to a tiny space at the back of her apartment. Gil sat and looked in the mirror. "Bring me into the 21st century."

"The ponytail should look totally Nam vet, but..." She lifted and parted sections of his thick auburn hair. "It's too thick." They looked in the mirror together. "And no gray, either."

"Well, give me some...and don't make me look like Custer."

After an hour, Cheyenne handed him a mirror."

He stared at himself in the mirror, lips pushed together. "Dang." Gil left with a power side cut, a la World War II, short with graying temples, courtesy of peroxide. Down on the street, he turned to Joe. "Hungry?"

"Always hungry, sir." They found a small outdoor eatery near the entry to Stearn's Wharf where they could see the tourists coming and going. "I didn't think tourists would be all over the place with the zombie scare."

Gil, not given to idle conversation on the best days, sat quietly with a sparkling water and a Reuben. Joe was mid-bite into a bacon burger when he stared into a group of girls coming off the wharf.

"Rachel?" Joe stood as he said it, transfixed, disbelieving.

"Joe!" Rachel's face was wide with wonder. "Joe. You're okay, you're alive!"

Joe reached her in two strides, hugging her like a drowning man. "Rache! Oh Rache, it is so good to see you."

"Pour some water on those two," laughed one of the girls in her gang.

"What are you doing here?" Joe and Rachel said at the same time. "You," he said. "Ladies first."

"There's an invitational volleyball tournament at Westmont College. Your turn."

"Umm, I'm thinking about joining the Coast Guard."

"Right." She studied his face as he squirmed and then she took pity. "You'd be stationed in Santa Barbara...?" she asked as Joe shrugged. "Because I'm graduating early and I'm going to start at Westmont this fall. I'm so done with high school."

"I'm looking into some other options, too," said Joe.

Rachel's friends started walking on. "The tournament is Saturday at three. Be there."

And she was gone. Joe stared after them and found his way back to the table.

Gil, of course, had seen it all. "That your girl?"

Joe slumped into his chair. "Only if stars notice tiny stick insects."

"She was friendly enough." Gil pushed a plate of fries toward Joe. "You're not much of a Romeo."

"I saw that movie," he said, sadly. "I think I *am* like him. He only wanted Juliet."

That got a half-smile from the commander, who now looked more hard-bitten with short hair. "Son, is she The One?"

Miserable, Joe nodded. "Since eighth grade when she moved to Seattle."

Gil took a swig, cleared his throat and began to sing. *"Some Enchaaaanted Evening..."* He had volume.

"That's gross!"

"Coyotes like it. They sing right along. *You may see a strangerrrr...*"

"Stop it! People are covering their ears!"

"Across a crowded roooom." The waiter made a face.

Gil pointed his finger in Joe's face. "If you don't set your sights on that girl with every ounce of your being, I will sing every time I see you goofing off. In the mess, in the Crisis Center. Anywhere. *Everywhere.* Do you roger?"

Joe raised his eyes. "Ma says women doing the choosing."

"So convince her that you are her best possible choice." Joe must not have looked convinced "...*And somehow you'll knooow.*" An oncoming couple crossed to the other side of the street.

Joe saluted. "Sir, yes, sir."

"Life is too long to let her slip away." Gil tapped his phone and called for a return car. Walking to the pick-up point, Joe said, "Do you think I should quote poetry below her window?"

Gil shook his head. "Never known that maneuver to work. Too many unknowns."

They passed a game store. "Look!" Joe pointed to the window. A large poster image of TezCat from *Inazuma Eleven* was right in front of them. TezCat in Anime, huge black eyes giving a thumbs-up, with the cartoon caption "Nice doo, Commander."

Gil bit out a very bad word. The car came and soon they were speeding over the waves in the RIB. Sirens sounded and they saw black smoke billowing from somewhere in the town center. Gil piloted it into open water and tapped Joe. "Keep it under 20 knots. I've got thinking to do....and keep an eye out for floaters."

As they left the dock Joe kept it slow, maybe next time he could let out the throttle. But he did think about Gil's challenge. *Maybe I can be the best student Bishop Diego Garcia High School has ever seen and impress Rachel. She did tell me to be at the tournament.* He could use Martin's trick of watching courses on You Tube, like Calculus, from Stanford. Then, go into class knowing most of what was coming. It had worked for Martin...or *maybe I'll be the dweeb in high school while college dudes are hitting on Rachel.*

He noticed Gil staring at him. "Sir?"

"I had the MP circle back and see if the caption had changed on the poster...there was no poster." He put his phone in a secured pocket. "Get your dang vest on and zip it!"

Joe "sink-like-a-stone" Comstock put on a sleek PFD and zipped it mostly up, then pushed the male/female belt buckle together. He steered the craft straight north toward the State Marine Conservation Area at Isla Vista. The *Ma Castro* lay beyond. About a half-mile off shore, Joe spotted something floating in the water. He cut the engine to a crawl and pointed at the object.

"That's one," Gil said. "Dang, with a tail."

"Are we going to lash it to the gunwales?" Joe said, with excitement.

"No. We are going to call for backup." Gil tapped in a number. Joe took a deep breath, but Gil cut him off with a pointing finger. "Neither of us is jumping in the water to rope it in."

Joe rolled his eyes. "But—"

"But," said Gil, "you think we should be more exciting."

"Exactly," said Joe. "The *Ma Castro's* boring."

He held up his hand as a call came through. "Commander Muirgen here. We have a floater. Our coordinates are—you can see us? Roger, out."

"Listen up, Fuzznuts." Gil was pointing his finger at Joe. "Sorry if our mission doesn't thrill you. Sorry if exploring the seafloor and seeking new life forms isn't enough. And —although this may not be exciting enough for you—we are currently spending all our resources on a minor threat that could possibly take out, oh, a million people or so." Gil jerked his thumb and took the wheel.

Joe gave up the helm so Gil could edge the craft next to the tail-toting Reanz. Jeans—ripped where the tail came out—a t-shirt with bra line, long hair. "It's a girl, sir!"

"Get your head back in the boat. It's getting choppy—and there's why!" Some monster motor yacht, half the length of the *Castro,* was barreling towards them from the west as the rescue boat approached from the east. "Idiot! I'll circle to hide the body."

Joe wasn't sure the yacht even saw them. The waves it created amplified the waves coming from the Coast Guard rescue boat that was fast approaching from the other direction. He held on.

We are the middle of a boat sandwich!

At the very last, the yacht's pilot saw them and made an abrupt sharp turn. A bikini babe who'd been dozing near the railing fell in.

Joe did not mean to rescue her. The wash from the yacht's steep turn, added to the amplified waves, popped him overboard. And he really didn't mean to land on the drowning woman. His life-vest inflated when he hit the water; he sucked in air and felt hands crawling up his body. Her hands clawed everywhere! Her feet were climbing his legs, pushing off his knees. The jacket attempted to keep Joe on his back with his head supported, but she kept pulling his head under. He tried to get air.

Now her knee was on his chest, somehow pushing down the safety zipper. Joe tried to push her off. A Coast Guard seaman was shoving a rescue pole at her, trying to get her to grab it. Joe got a glimpse of a second man adjusting a facemask and falling backwards with a scuba tank.

Another gasp for air.

The belt on the life preserver snapped. She was pulling it off him!

Then he was free.

Chapter fifteen

Then he was sinking.

He kicked, trying to surface, trying for air. Bikini babe's last move was to use his head as a stepping stone toward the pole and Joe went under into the gloom of the coastal kelp forest. His legs kicked; his arms pulled. He went only down...again. *MomDadMartinMomDadMartin,MomDadMartin, MomDadMartin. Mom Dad Martin. Mom, Dad, Martin. Mom, Dad, Martin. Mom...Dad...Martin. Mom...*

Lungs bursting, he felt himself rising! The surface lightened, the kelp strands brightened. He looked toward his rescuer: Martin!

He drank in draughts of air, unable to stop as his brother pushed him into the arms of the rescue diver, who instantly put Joe's hands on a rope attached to the boat. When he looked around, Martin was gone. He tried to go under but the diver pushed him up.

NO! He let go of the rope and kicked all-out toward where Martin had last been...and swam into the drifting, face-down Reanz girl they had yet to lash to the rescue boat.

Gross!

Her arms floated over him like seaweed, like a drunken date, and then she bit him.

The diver, safely suited in 6mm neoprene, succeeded in finally getting Joe to the RB's boarding ladder. Another crew member pulled him aboard and slapped an occlusive dressing on the shoulder wound—not filet mignon this time—and sat him on a bench with a blanket.

Martin? It was Martin.

The bikini girl threw up near his feet; the vomit reeked of gin. Joe just moved his feet.

That had to be Martin. Martin's alive! He's a merm, a Swimmer. Like Ma. Okay. So why…?

His mind went where he didn't want it to go. *Martin is a True. I don't even know what a True looks like*…But he did. His first day on the cutter, Melusine said Trues have gills and their legs are fused and the tails are permanent. And the burly seaman said they're kind of bluish. Joe stared at the horizon.

Soon, Gil was leading him down to sickbay in the *Ma Castro*, again. "Son, you are a pain in my rear."

Joe didn't care. "I want to talk to my mother."

Gil studied his face and nodded. "Roger that."

Melusine came in, her face grim. "Bitten by a Reanz? A Reanz floating in the water, meaning *you* were in the water." She shook her hands. "I don't know which one of you to slap first!" Gil was on his phone.

"I saw Martin. He kept me from drowning." Joe studied her face. "So you knew. You both knew!"

"Call. His. Mother."

"On it," said Gil.

Joe said nothing as Melusine repeated the actions of before: culture, antibiotics, new dressing, vital signs. The doctor opened her mouth to speak.

He stared beyond her. "Don't bother. I live or I die. Three days, right?"

She shook her head slowly back and forth, crossing her arms.. "Young Joe, Magnet-for-Trouble, how did you live *this* long?"

He looked at her for an instant. "Doc? Don't tell Luz Marina, okay?"

She nodded. Joe waited for Gil, holding it in. He came back in, his arms behind his back.

Now Joe stood, his anger potent and rising. "You spoke to her, right? Let me tell you both: I've had it. I've had it! Ma's dead; she's not dead. Martin's dead; he's not dead. Nobody tells me a freaking thing!" His shouting made him cough up some sea goop. "What crap did she tell you?"

"She said." Gil paused to lift his eyebrows. "Let the boys work it out. I'm busy."

#

Joe was in his second day in quarantine, and for no good reason. He was no threat to anyone unless he died and attacked someone. *Gil put me here 'cause I'm so angry...no, he put me in here so the crew doesn't have to see their pet lab rat get sick and die.* Joe stared out the round window, willing Martin to pop his head above the waves. *Ma knew, did Dad?*

Then he lay down. He didn't feel well and the fever was climbing. Did she know he was in quarantine? "Not enough data" as Dad would say. Joe ignored his craving for fish heads, threw his arm over his eyes and fell asleep.

"Wake up, son." Gill was opening the door. Next, he carried a chair into the sickbay. "Company."

Too miserable to complain, Joe opened his eyes. "Martin?!"

The two burly seamen gently placed his 6-foot-1-inch brother in the chair. His tail was charcoal and blue swirls, like a mackerel. The three men stood behind the lab window.

Joe forced himself to sitting. He felt worse than ever. "Martin."

"Hey bro...I wanted to see you, in case."

"In case I die?" Joe tried to take in all the changes in his big brother's body. He couldn't help but stare.

"This was a mistake." Martin waved to the men.

"No! Don't go! Wait, I won't die, I promise. I feel about the same as the last time. Stay, Martin. I'm sorry I looked. Please...please."

"I'm Martin the Monster."

"I'm cool with tails. Everybody here has tails."

Martin shook his head. "And blue? And padded with fat? And gills. Let's not forget the gills!" Martin raised an arm. On the side of his chest, along each rib, were folded flaps of skin.

Joe felt helpless. "I thought you were dead, bro."

"I am dead." At that, he swung away toward the door and said no more as the muscular men performed a two-man carry.

"You gotta come back, bro. Come back!"

But Martin left. Gil stood at the door, shaking his head, his face cut with sadness. Joe felt more miserable, more sick. He started trembling and fell back on his bunk. Soon, he had a cool washcloth on his head and Melusine putting a thermometer in his ear.

"One oh two point seven," she said.

Joe turned on his stomach and tried not to cry. "I'm gonna die and nobody's here. Martin said it was a mistake and Ma's too busy. What sort of family is this?" he sobbed. "I don't want to die by myself, Doc. Don't let me die by myself."

"I'm family," said Gil. "I won't leave." He pulled the chair to Joe's side and placed his hand on his shoulder. Joe relaxed and fell into a restless, fevered sleep.

Later, he opened his eyes in the electronic half-light. "Martin?"

"It's me, Fuzznuts. Feel better?"

"I want to." He watched Gil stand and stretch. "I dreamed of a floating zombie and Martin coming out of the kelp...oh. It's true."

Gil put a fresh cool cloth on his head. "I'll tell you about my little ranch. Sound good?"

"Hmmm," said Joe.

"I'd lived through about a century's worth of bloodshed on the Continent. Didn't think it would ever change, or end. The Prussians fought the French, the Swedes, the Spanish, the Italians, the Russians, and especially their fellow Germans. Treaties, intrigues. Battles and blood. But I had a reputation of being a river scout and a German prince, Maximilian, heard about me. He was a famous explorer—brought back the first images of Brazil and its natives. Karl Bodmer, actually; he was the artist. The prince made money on the aquatints and decided to find Indians in the northern American."

"What year?" Joe yawned.

"That was 1833. We started in Baltimore, went overland through the Lehigh Valley and down the Ohio River out of Pittsburgh. Smoky even then. We followed Lewis and Clark's route until Montana. They went high. We went low on the Missouri."

"You met Indians?"

"Many, some of them not particularly happy to see us. Lewis and Clark had come through in 1806. They didn't take with being told their lands were now belonged to the Big Chief in Washington. But they didn't mind sitting for

Herr Bodmer. Came out in their finery and paints and quills, showed off their dances. Drums and flutes of sorts. The men would shout and stomp, the women rustled and rattled their beads and shells and..."

Joe opened his eyes. It was still dark. Gil was still at his side. "I fell asleep, huh?"

"Yep." Gil stuck a straw in his mouth. " Didn't know I was such a boring storyteller."

Joe swallowed. "No! It's just that...you know..."

"Shall I continue?"

"Please."

"As relates to Golden Eagle ranch, a son of the chief of the Blackfoot fell into a very rough section of the Upper Missouri. I fished him out, so to speak."

"You flashed your tail?"

"You betcha. Flummoxed the Prince, and Dreidoppel, his servant, fell over. But I highly impressed the chief. He offered me his daughter, Peeta. Golden Eagle."

Joe could hear Gil's heart sighing.

"Well, she tried her best to look submissive and all, but when I asked—through our interpreter—if I should ask for a horse, she glared like an angry eagle. I put up three fingers. She put up five—on one hand. Then five on the other hand, and five again. I am the chief's daughter, she said, looking first at her father, then at me. I reckoned she was right and I looked at the chief...and we were a team from that moment.

"The Prince said the words, and then the medicine man did his thing, and Herr Karl made a sketch. The women found the match hilarious: the Eagle had caught herself a Fish."

"Then you...?"

"The Prince let me go. I'd weirded him out with the tail. They found another scout, I guess. Old Maxi said I was too rich for his blood what with my herd of ponies. A good man...you're starting to fade again, Fuzznuts, so I'll cut this short. We stayed with the tribe for a bit, then my beauty and I went southeast along the Yellowstone, before there was Wyoming and I started ranching. Didn't know one end of a cow from the other..."

Chapter sixteen

"*Mon cheri*, Gilbert tells me you are now very sick." Joe nodded into the Messenger screen. "He said Martin had rescued you, but you fought. I was more 'appy than worried. Now Gilbert says...one of them bit you! And this place where I am, I can check emails no more than once a day."

"Hard work, saving the oceans," said Joe, too miserable to be resentful.

"It means nothing." Tears began to run down her face.

"Ma, don't cry." She put her face in her hands and sobbed. Joe had to make her stop. "I was lucky the first time, Ma. No reason to think I won't be this time, huh?"

His mother wiped her tears with her hands and attempted to smile. "I will tell you this to make you strong. You are your father's favorite. Not that he loves Martin less—no, the love of a son is a bond till death—but you are the bone of his bone, the flesh of his flesh."

"'Putting the stock in Comstock'. I won't tell." Joe sighed. "Ma, Martin is a True. Did Dad know?"

She found a tissue and dabbed her eyes. "It was his idea to let the world think the tides 'ad carried him away. Martin came to see you?" his mother asked.

"Yeah," said Joe. "He said it was a mistake."

"Oh, *mon grand,* he did not mean you. He means his misfortunes."

"Why do you keep having kids, Ma, when..." He watched her rub fresh tears from her eyes. "I'm sorry."

"I love to love, Joseph. Perhaps I am selfish."

"Ma, I'm falling asleep. Call me later?"

"Whenever Gil calls me. Sleep, *mon cheri*. I will sit by the phone."

Joe woke up. True to his word, Gil had remained at his side. "Why didn't you tell her?

Gil frowned. "It's my job to protect her. She's safe where she is."

"Can I have a beer, then?"

Gil reached into the tiny refrigerator and pulled out two Dos Equis. "Bad precedent." As he was twisting the cap, Melusine appeared at the window. "Temp first," she said, brooking no nonsense.

Gil and Joe looked at other and shrugged. Joe put the thermometer in his ear. "One oh one." The three smiled. "And my hands aren't shaking!"

"What do you think, Mellie?"

"I think that he had a bigger immune response this time because of the first infection. I will need more blood before we can be certain."

Joe extended his arm. "Lab rat, at your service...I can still have the beer. It's good after a fever, right, Doc?"

"You are not dying and Gatorade will serve you as well."

Joe sighed as Gil obediently placed the beer back in the fridge. She scrubbed her hands to the elbows and came in to draw blood. "Would you like me to call your mother?"

"Maybe just a text. I'd still like to sleep...and I want to see Martin again."

Gil looked between them, then nodded. "I'll do what I can," he said, pulling out his phone to read a new text.

Finishing the blood draw, Melusine said, "If you haven't succumbed to any other grisly death, I'll need more in four days."

"No Martin today." Gil handed Joe a Gatorade. "The place with the poster? It burned to the ground."

#

The next morning, well rested and more electrolytes restored with an orange juice, Joe showered. He felt a small dimple under his right armpit. *Hmm, did I pull a muscle? Could have, with bikini girl.*

When he went to the mess for food, Captain Bannerman stood and started clapping and the rest of the crew followed suit. Joe, embarrassed, gave a lame salute and went to the bagel station. He sat with the burly guys, Afro-American Hunter and Heinz-57 Kyle, both sporting massive tattooed arms.

"Hey, little buddy," said Kyle, "you're one tough dude."

"You guys only like me for my blood."

"He's scorning our true affection," said Hunter, "I think I am offended."

Kyle said, "Hunter and I think we should be your fulltime bodyguards. Keep you out of trouble." Hunter nodded.

"Bodyguards for the lab rat?" said Joe.

"Lab rat? Dude," said Hunter to Kyle, "that makes us the Rat Patrol!" When he saw Gil approaching, he stood. "Commander, Seaman Miller and I are volunteering to be bodyguards for Joe here, sir."

"Sit," said Gil, considering the offer. "I'll talk to the captain. Either of you working the Crisis Center?"

"Negatory, sir," they said together.

"Joe?" Gil said.

"Rachel?"

Gil made a face of understanding. "You two can be invisible when needed?" When they nodded, Joe sighed, and Gil continued. "There is a 'maneuver' this Saturday at 3pm. I will give you details later. But right now, Joe needs a ride over to Peggy's Bar. Affirmative?"

"Sir, yes, sir," said the sailors.

"Joe, Martin will see you when you get there. He is not a happy camper."

"Thank you, sir." Joe studied his bagel and eggs as Gil went over to the Captain's table. "I never know whether to call him 'Sir' or 'Gil.'"

"Can't mess up with 'sir,'" said Kyle. "Eat up, Lab Rat. We're not leaving till you eat a good breakfast."

Joe searched their faces. "And what's with 'Fuzznuts'?"

"Military tradition. We don't mess with it."

"I was Fuzznuts until a younger sailor came aboard," said Hunter. "Military tradition."

#

The RIB bouncing over the waves, Joe kept warm in Hunter's XXL Coast Guard jacket. "Where's Peggy's Bar?" he asked.

"Top secret," said Kyle.

Okay, at least they didn't blindfold me. And as far as I can see, we're headed toward the Channel Islands.

Squinting without sunglasses, Joe reflected on the changes of life: two weeks ago he had been alone in the world, now he had Martin—sort of—and Ma and Gil. And two he-man bodyguards sticking to him like duct tape.

Forty minutes later, the RIB edged up to a rocky ledge just inside a cave. "Back there," said Hunter. "About 90 feet."

Joe saw no signs of habitation. Light was from a few pit holes in the rock above. Even that light faded as he came farther in. He jumped when he made out Martin seated on a step, his mackerel tail submerged to the knee.

"Ah," said his brother. "Welcome to my lair. I am the Great High Commander, Sultan of the Surf."

"Wacko of the Waves?" said Joe.

"King of the Kelp. Fish fear me."

"How about dolphins?"

"No way, they probe everywhere. Worse than aliens," said Martin. "So, you made it." His voice held no emotion.

"That's good, right?" Joe wished his brother would smile or something.

Martin looked at him. He nodded. "Yeah, that's good."

"Is this where you live?" The space was primitive, a wide slab of thick foam—a bed? And trough sink with a spigot. About 10 feet above this space he saw the familiar blue glow of the computer screen.

Martin ignored his question. "Fill me in on 'Joe's exciting life.'"

"I figure you'd know it all," said Joe. "All the details like Ma didn't die and you didn't wash out to sea."

"You're going to stand there on your two good legs and whine?"

Joe kept quiet; he never could win an argument with Martin.

"Let's start with the rescue," said his brother. "Do you have any idea what the Mavericks is, the place you went down? In February and March, that spot gets sixty to eighty foot waves. It's risky even in good conditions."

Joe spread his hands. "How was I supposed to know?"

"Maybe research your navigation chart? You're the great sailor in the family. There's a surfing contest there every February; it's famous for its waves and for taking out surfers. Three of my Trues were seriously injured."

"From the waves?" said Joe.

"No, from the seafloor. It's like a massive cheese grater—think 'big rocks'—all the way to the cliff face."

"Are they okay?" Martin nodded. "I guess I'm stupid, huh?"

"Yeah. And the boat's in pieces."

"It was Dad's."

"Meaning it would be magically protected? Did you ever wonder how we found you in the middle of a storm? There was a GPS tracker on the hull," said Martin.

"I saw it," said Joe, "but I figured Dad had placed it."

"It was placed by one of Mother's minions."

"A moperative." Martin gave a half smile at that; Joe clutched the thin thread of favor.

"Gil and his crew tried to get to the sloop carrying O2 tanks for you. We got there first. There were hundreds of us, Swimmers and Trues. The waves were seventy, eighty feet high and fifty feet wide. It was like being on the mother of all trampolines in a rug cleaner during a tornado."

"Could you see me?"

"I could sense you. Mother had us watching out for you since you left the Sound. But I knew where you were."

Joe looked at his brother's face, noted that his eyes were farther spaced than before, noted that his beard was more sparse. He loved him with all his heart. "I love you, bro. I owe you my life."

Martin looked like he'd been punched in the gut. "Time to go, little Joe."

Joe froze. "I have to go? Can I come back?"

Martin sat with his eyes closed and waved him away with his hands. Joe walked the half the way back to the RIB. He turned for one last look. But his brother was not there. "And Dad?" he hollered. "What do you know about Dad?"

No answer.

Hunter and Kyle were actually quiet on the way back, just when Joe wished they'd talk their usual nonsense. With the *Ma Castro* in view, he spilled his guts. "Do you guys think I'm stupid?"

"In general or in particular?" said Hunter.

"Ah, in particular. The whole rescue thingy."

"Oh," said Kyle. "The 'rescue thingy'. Yep, that was stupid."

"Because I didn't know about the Mavericks?"

"Because," said Hunter, "you didn't know about the winds, the barometer, the radar, nothing. You just vibed out, "Nothing can happen to me"."

"Yeah," said Kyle, "that was a bona fide cluster cuss."

"But it gave *us* something to do. The rescue boats ate our foam that night!" Hunter patted Joe on the back. "If most people didn't leave their brains at the dock, we'd have a boring life."

"And in general?" said Joe, hopefully.

"Do not push your luck, Ratty."

Chapter seventeen

News from Gorilla Glass:

<u>National Enquirer</u>: Zombies stole my job! Bigfoot is a zombie!, Muslim zombie terrorists!, Infected coyotes reanimate in Oregon!, I was probed by zombies!

Democratic National Committee floats forgiveness for student loans for zombies. IRS fights back, says no loan forgiveness for zombies.

Immigrant activists say FHF is a conspiracy to scare off immigrants.

All fevers-of-unknown-origin are given a mandatory three-day hospital stay. The ACLU says personal freedoms infringed.

When Joe returned to the Crisis Center, the mood of the place had changed. "We know the agent! The Doctora just told us," said Red.

"It's a virus placed in a bacterium," said the corpsman.

"Placed? It's new, man-made?" said Joe.

"She thinks so," continued Red. "And—and this is huge—that little bullet goes into a worm!"

"Ewww. How do we get it? How did *I* get it?" said Joe. Both men shrugged. "Is the worm a shrimp?" said Joe. Both shrugged again.

"Joe! Luz!" Gil was waving them to join him. Joe and Luz Marina followed him into his tiny office. "Got Finn on the line. Sounds semi-hysterical. Okay, Finn, We're on speaker phone. Start again, go slow."

"There's a large black bird with a suitcase sitting on top of my security light!"

Joe momentarily reflected that after the past two weeks a bird with a suitcase wasn't all that surprising.

"Where is the suitcase?" asked Luz Marina.

And she's not surprised, either.

"On his back," Finn shouted. "And did I say he dropped a note? He dropped a handwritten note—in exceptionally fine Italic script—from a Lady Michi."

"Ah!" said la doctora.

"You know her?" said Gil.

She gave a dainty shrug. "I know of her. In Mexico, we call her Teomichi"

"And," said Finn, his voice getting high and tight, "she's asking permission to visit with her entourage! An *entourage!*"

"They will be in the suitcase," said Luz Marina.

As Gil gave his usual studious frown, Finn shouted, "What do I do?"

"*Muy simple.* Treat them like royalty."

As she walked away, Joe caught up. "Luz Marina, do I have worms?"

"Ah, you heard. No. No worms for you, *corazón*, only for primary victims."

Now Gil was standing with them, off his phone. "Fuzznuts, this is your detail."

"Huh, what?!"

"Your house—" Joe shook his head as Gil kept talking. "You go help Finn; be a good host. I'm sure you learned something from your folks."

"And the Rat Patrol?" Joe added with desperation.

Gil puzzled over the name, and then let out a chuckle. "Ooh, they'll love this." He nodded. "I'll send them."

Joe wanted to hug him, but resisted.

"*Excelente,*" smiled Luz Marina. "I will come in two days to the house of your mama and take your blood and give my respects."

"Who is Lady What's-Her-Name?"

"Teomichi is *la patrona* of Lake Chapala."

Gil was quicker than Joe. "Is she a 'swimmer'?"

The Mexican geneticist shook her head. "No, no. She is a fish...not that you could know."

#

In short order, Joe and company were deposited on the sidewalk of his mother's house. Tall, lanky Finn looked like a man trying very hard not to explode. "They're out back. At the pool. This is a nightmare, a security nightmare! Take over," he yelled, arms waving. "I have to get the black side panels up...and my drone screen isn't functioning. This can't get out, this can't get out," Finn muttered as he walked away.

"Alright, Ratty," said Kyle, "let's get this going".

"Do you mind that I got you into this?" said Joe, worried.

"Rat Patrol, Go-fer Patrol, doesn't matter to me."

Hunter nodded in agreement as they took charge, striding through the house to the back patio and pool. Joe could have collapsed with relief. Maybe someday he'd be fearless, too. Kyle shook his head as they walked the perimeter of the property. Finn had raised the black security screens behind the tall venerable cypress trees that lined the property north and south. The neighbors could see nothing. Behind was the house and west, of course, the ocean.

None of them were quite sure what they were looking for. They were looking at the back of a good-sized cormorant, for sure, thought Joe.

They walked around it. The glossy green-black seabird sat flat on its webbed feet, wings spread. They watched it nudge a tiny wicker suitcase into the shade with its beak. Satisfied with its position, the bird looked up at each of them in turn with its bright turquoise eyes.

"Gentlemen," it said, tipping its beak to the ground, "Please take a seat."

"Whoa," whispered Joe.

"We'll stand," said Hunter. "A bird with an English accent."

Using the small hook on its beak, the cormorant tapped the latch open and gracefully opened the case. "Done that before," said Kyle. Next, it spread a woven cloth, then used its pointer feathers to gently lift figures the size of toy soldiers onto the cloth.

"A dog?" said Hunter.

"Maybe," said Kyle. "Dude, I love my job."

The dog expanded unevenly. Its legs popped out one at a time, like someone blowing up a latex glove. Next, its body swelled and a head bulged out. Last, it shook itself from nose to tail.

"That's one ugly Chihuahua. Look at them bug eyes...Ow!" Hunter swatted at the dog with its teeth sunk in his calf. "What! You a racist dog?"

"One in every crowd," said Kyle, his lips barely moving.

"I am Chihuahua most beautiful," she said, growling with her teeth bared.

"Okay, okay. I'm sorry, didn't mean to hurt your feelings." The dog put her small nose in the air and tiptoed over to the woven cloth and sat watching the next figure expand.

"Shoulda known, dude," Kyle whispered to Hunter, his lips scarcely moving.

"Livin' the dream," said Hunter, rubbing the bite.

'Next' was a beautiful woman. High cheek bones set in a perfect oval face which highlighted eyes that were dramatic and dark. Her clothes were chic and austere accenting the golden velvet of her skin. A deep breath and she expanded fully, from her simply clad feet to her severe tight ponytail. Stretching, she looked at the Rat Patrol. "I require a lap top...and water for us." The men looked at Joe from both sides.

"Yes, ma'am," he said and scrambled toward the kitchen.

When he returned with three tumblers, two bowls and a pitcher of ice water, the last two members of the *entourage* were sitting in lounge chairs. The bird was unpacking smart phones and the dog—now with tiny hands where paws had been—distributed them.

"Thank you, dahling. Filtered?" said the stylish blond in the deepest voice he'd ever heard from a woman.

"Organic," said Joe, thinking of Rachel. One of her favorite nonsense lines.

"Lovely," said the redhead with curls. Lady Michi nodded at him. The dog lapped delicately. The bird paused from its dipping and splashing to whisper, "A laptop, young master, if you would."

Joe found Finn basically hiding in the cellar.

"A laptop? Madame Queen desires a laptop? All right, all right, I'll bring one up. We have three beds to make, you know. And we need food in the house. These people are beyond belief!"

Joe presented the laptop as regally as he could, but still she waited. The bird made horizontal motions with its wing feathers. Joe brought over a poolside table, looking to the bird for direction. Finally getting it right, Joe retired to his bodyguards who were standing at a powerful at-ease.

"The blonde is hitting on me," said Hunter, lips hardly moving.

"She's skanky," said Kyle. "Look at her hands, they're all muddy."

"My mother warned me about fish," Hunter continued in a low voice.

"Seriously?" said Joe.

"Yeah, dude, they're cold."

"Ooh, tall, dark and haaandsome," called the blond, pointing to Hunter. "And vat *you* do?"

Hunter stood with his mouth zipped shut.

"Oh, Zima! Have you no pride?" said the redhead. "Take a bath! You're an absolute mess."

"I just voke up, Bunya! Is barely time for nap, three months. Three months in my beloved Desna." Zima sighed. "River mud is so good for ze skin. Daahling?" called the blond, pointing to Hunter. "I need manicure. You help me?"

Hunter crossed his arms, refusing to move.

"We're on it, ma'am," said Kyle. He dialed the phone and handed it to Joe. "The Commander knows everybody."

Joe asked and Gil did know a manicurist. Joe took a chance. "Do you think, sir, that Martin could come over? He wouldn't stand out in this crowd." Joe handed the phone back. "I'll make the beds."

His fearless bodyguards blocked him. "We'll make the beds."

Stuck, Joe waited to be ordered around. He watched the little dog wander, sniffing the trees down to the edge of the lawn. *Dog toilet, maybe?* The great lady was absorbed in the computer screen. And the blonde and redhead, now adorned with wide-brimmed hats and sunglasses, seem to be glued to their reclining loungers, poolside. The cormorant was busy however, standing on one webbed foot and scratching a pen on paper with the other. Finished, the bird waddled over to him with a dignified air. Somehow, the creature had tamed the silly, white, mating-season quills that stood out on its cheeks by sweeping them back into distinguished temples.

Is that a bowtie? Joe stared at the pale patch of feathers on his throat. "Are you a butler?"

"Indeed I am, young master. And I have compiled a small list of food and drink items. Perhaps you would be kind enough to have them delivered?" Joe nearly dropped the paper that was the size of a postage stamp. And as he held on it expanded, somehow, to a 6 x 8 inch sheet.

Now, the dog stood next to the bird. "Please," she said, "to read list."

"Burgers and French fries, four orders, with Coca-Cola," he looked at them. They nodded. "One dozen limes. A container of heavy cream. Lemonade, bread, and wines. Fine crackers, caviar. French roast for espresso." They nodded.

"Do you have a name?" Joe asked the bird.

The dog answered. "Bird is called Otis. Lady say, Bird go up, bird go down. Like elevator." The bird gave a formal bow.

Otis continued. "This fine Chihuahua is Chantico." The dog bowed her head, her plain leather collar sliding up and down.

"A pleasure to meet you both," Joe said. *I should get a medal.* Ma was the Manners Police, saying manners—not love—made the world go round, like some sort of cosmic grease. *Maybe she's right.* He waved the list, nodded, and fled into the house.

After a discussion with Finn and the burly guys, it was decided Hunter and Joe would deploy for rations. "The wine cellar is adequate; we have espresso. And I'll have the burgers and fries delivered...for all of us? The rest you can get here." Finn wrote the address on the list.

"On it," said Hunter, skirting the Chihuahua who growled whenever he got close. "We're out of here, Rat Boy."

Everyone had burgers and fries by the poolside. Joe found himself doing most of the serving, but the last thing he was going to do was complain to the Rat Patrol. Otis's blue eyes were crazy—they glowed like LEDs and were circled by tiny turquoise dots! He dipped each French fry in ketchup and popped it up and into his beak like a herring. Chantico daintily nibbled her burger, then attacked a mound of fries as big as her head. Stomach distended in a happy glut, she fell on her side, panting. Finn had finally joined the entourage, expounding the merits of his wine cellar to Zima and Bunya.

The doorbell rang. Hunter answered the front door and just returned to the patio. "Here," the seaman said, handing a business card to the cormorant. "There's a kid on a bike waiting for a message."

Otis looked up at Joe. "Have you a salver?" Finn was already walking into the kitchen and returned with a small silver plate. The bird laid the business card carefully in the middle and waddle-walked over to his mistress.

"You may read it," she said.

"He-whose-slaves-we-are presents his card and his best wishes for your health. He inquires at what time you should like to go eat at the taco truck."

While the blonde and redhead made knowing female comments, Teomichi calmly said that she would be expecting him at two in the afternoon the following day. Hunter took that message to the door and, when he came back, told Kyle that he had already called the Commander about "He-whose-slaves-we-are". "Sounds like a real popular dude."

Joe, then, went down the steps and found the billiard room. "Whoa!"

In front of him was a splendid antique pool table. Dark wood, webbed leather pockets with tassels. Joe reverently stroked the rails and the green felt. *Slate, real slate under this baby.* He barely pushed a ball over the surface and saw it veered just a bit. He checked the floor. *Ah, it's the floor, good to know.* He picked up a cue and racked the balls. Gently, patiently, Joe set up shots, studied the diamond insets on the rails, and blocked out the world. Pool or billiards, the geometry and skill always drew him in. At first, Dom the Dad had taken him to Brufsky's Arcade, but the noisy lights of pinball didn't appeal. Dad sneaked him into the bar where he chalked his first cue stick. Later, the back room of Brufsky's became his refuge, the place he spent his allowance.

Joe missed a shot as Hunter and Kyle pounded down the steps to angry voices. Martin's voice!

And a different voice.

Chapter eighteen

Joe navigated down the dark interior steps carved into the cliff. In a more sophisticated and finished space than Peggy's Bar, Martin was shaking his fist across a crack in the seafloor at what had to be a female True. "I told you not to come. Go! Leave me alone." The bluish female, sleek with no waist, long hair over flat breasts, leaned in across from him, squealing in an unknown language. She was clearly angry.

"I don't care about the Director," Martin shouted back. "Stop coming around!"

In a maneuver of exquisite athleticism, the female made a partial handstand and smacked his brother onto his back with her powerful tail. A few parting squeals and she was gone. Hunter and Kyle, both in their no-nonsense, arms-crossed stance looked at the brothers and left them alone.

"I hate her." Martin was breathing deeply. "She's the reason we crawled on land. I hate her, I hate her!"

"What did she do?" said Joe.

"She keeps coming on to me."

"That's good, right?"

"I am not into casual fish sex." Joe felt totally out of his element. He did not want to hear whatever was coming next. "She's changing," continued Martin, "into a male."

"How—*what*?!

"I don't know! It might be normal fish behavior. Gling says he's gone back and forth a few times depending on the population count. But she's getting bigger. I'm not doing a good job getting her pregnant, obviously. Mother selected her because she didn't think Eemee would be too choosy."

"Mother?"

"Precisely. Hand-picked by our own loving mother."

"Holy crap!" said Joe.

"Right you are. A totally physical relationship dictated by the Director. But being the Director's son has no pull when your job is to make little baby merms."

"She's kinda cute, maybe?" said Joe. As he spoke, the entourage above ground suddenly became so normal.

"You throw her a fish, then. I can't. I just can't anymore. And she is so stupid. And boring! I've tried—from Mozart to *Jackass*, nothing. *Funniest Home Videos*? Zip. Some of them are bright enough, like Gling. He gets arithmetic and time, digital and analog. But Eemee, 'swim north till sunset, turn west at the steam vent', that is the best she can do."

Martin exhaled. He scooted back from the water and rested on pillows propped on the cave wall. His eyes drilled into Joe's. "Why do you want me around?"

"I keep hoping you'll stop being grumpy."

"You keep hoping the 'old Martin' will show up." His brother shook his head. "I wanted to be Governor, Brother. I wanted to be a policy wonk. I wanted to go to Harvard!"

"There are three beautiful women here. Luz Marina says they're fish, but they just look like beautiful women. I thought maybe you'd be comfortable here."

"Oh little Joe, more women will not make my life better."

"Could you just stay tomorrow?"

Martin nodded. "Yeah, I'll stay tomorrow. Go to bed."

Chapter nineteen

"Open the door, Rat boy!"

That was Joe's wake-up call. He had made his way to the library couch sometime in

the night. In front of him, the Rat Patrol was carrying Martin in a chair hold. "It is that tail made of lead, dude?"

"Solid muscle. Jealous?"

After placing him in a lounger by the pool, Hunter spoke to Joe. "We served breakfast to the fish. You do lunch."

Joe fell back on to couch and rolled over, taking a pillow with him. He tried to absorb yesterday. *Otis, Chantico, Teomichi, Zima, Bunya. Holy crap—inflatable fish! And Finn. And Martin with his super gross girlfriend!* He felt bad. *Ma really is a piece of work.*

Eventually, he dragged himself to the kitchen. Wearing his other clean T-shirt, he pushed a hand through his hair and said to Kyle, "This good enough?"

Kyle shrugged and rewarded Joe with a spinach smoothie mixed with protein powder.

"Can't I just have a bagel?"

"Yeah, with the smoothie."

Joe gave up on trying to suck up the spinach paste and gulped it down. *I'm still their lab rat.* "And when's lunch? It's already 10 o'clock." His answer was another shrug.

Joe and the seamen looked out the back French doors onto the pool and patio. Teomichi was on her laptop with Chantico at her feet. But the fish ladies were being anointed by someone vaguely familiar. "Is that Cheyenne?" he said. "She gave the commander his new doo."

"Affirmative," said Kyle. "But that might be classified information, dude."

Joe inwardly sighed. He watched her pat a thick green clay mask on Zima's face. "All done," sang Cheyenne, placing thick cucumber slices over her eyes. "Now, put those pretty little fingers in these cute little bowls," she said, placing bowls of soapy water beneath Zima's fingers. "And we'll get to that manicure in a bit. Now, I'm back upstairs to your friend." As she passed the men, she mouthed the words, "pain in the rear", pointing upstairs.

Joe decided not to take shower until he knew where everybody was. He scanned the back of the property and there was Otis, perched on top of a security light.

"They don't tan. They don't burn," said Hunter, frowning. Joe assumed he meant the fish ladies.

"Have you checked out their eyelashes", said Kyle. "They look like fish skeletons, I mean, who has eyelashes that stick out like tail fins?"

Hunter said, "They're fish. I called my mom. She said this bunch takes men's money."

Kyle continued. "They look 28, but they seem really old."

Joe spoke up. "I googled 'Rusalka'. They're spirits. They lure men to the river banks and drown them."

"That's old school," said Hunter. "Now they marry them and take them for every nickel."

Finn came up from his lair. "I am worried about drones coming over. I'd rather shoot them out of the sky with a laser," he said, peering up at the sky. "But the Director wants us to be invisible. And the ever-so-wise Santa Barbara council allows them to 350 feet. I've been wanting to try out this little number forever."

They followed Finn out to Martin's recliner, the nearest one to the kitchen. As his brother lifted his laptop, Finn unfolded a holographic image of swim trunks, knees, hairy legs and feet, giving the image of a normal human man. "Ho ho. Take that, drones!"

Joe pulled up a chair, taking in the *entourage*. Hunter was now talking to Otis, still perched on the pole; Teomichi was looking at Martin. She was asking Martin if he could help her with a particular email server for a particular name, the one on the business card she handed him. "You know Howard Buffett?!" said Martin, incredulous. The great lady smiled at him, obviously impressed with his knowledge base.

Business as usual. Martin knows everything. I guess if I loved to read...and sit and sit and sit.

"He's the rich dude, right?" said Joe. *Either that, or he's the Margaritaville guy.*

Her eyes fixed upon Martin's as she answered Joe. "He is the rich dude's son. The farmer. We correspond."

I should know better. I should know better than to ever say anything. He watched Martin tinker with her keyboard and then hand it back. She smiled and completed her email. "Chantico, the feet. He comes at two."

Joe looked at the dog. "Are you a totem animal?"

That brought a cheerless yip from the Chihuahua who lifted sorrowful brown eyebrows. "I am a slave, no totem, I was a princess."

"Everybody say they are princess," said Zima.

"I *was* a princess," she said, growling. Teomichi snapped her fingers in warning. "I forgot to fast." She hung her little head. "That is not the truth: I did not want to fast. Who was I not to be grateful?" Chantico continued, looking up into the wall of trees. "The life of the corn, the fish, the rain, the water—all come from the gods. Maybe from a finger of a god, maybe a head. *Tal vez,* a foot like He-whose-slaves-we-are. All life springs from their sacrifices. But I was not grateful. No. I ate. Now I paint the toes of my lady."

"Who turned you into a dog?" said Hunter.

Chantico did not answer. Instead, she gave a tiny bark to her mistress who touched her head. Joe watched her paws and claws become hands and fingers. *Whoa.* She went to work painting Teomichi's toenails dark jade.

When Cheyenne approached the dog growled. "She's all yours, sister, I have enough to do," said the beautician.

"Do you think Dad's out there?" Joe asked his brother. "Away on some secret Wide World of Fish business?"

Martin took a chug of chocolate milk that Kyle had left. "We don't know where he is. None of his DNA was found in the Canal. Luz had us testing the bottom feeders right away...after we got a DNA sample."

Joe started. "The break in! My bedroom window was forced open. I couldn't figure out what was taken."

"Dad's toothbrush. Plus my team still does daily swim-throughs."

"That's cool; you're a leader."

"I guess," said Martin.

"I guess it's good I'm finding out *now*," said Joe.

"*Here* we go," said his brother who took a breath and then closed his lips. Joe turned to see Kyle standing with a finger to his lips. "Later," Martin said.

It was decided that lunch would be at 2, Teomichi not caring if they ate in front of her. Joe carted out fancy toasts and caviar, and wines from Finn's cellar. Hunter set down ice waters for the fish, Martin, Cheyenne, the "service animals" and themselves.

Without discernable cause, Chantico growled at Hunter and charged, running under Joe's feet and jumping thigh-high aiming to inflict maximum damage. The bowl and fruit Joe was carrying went airborne and Joe tripped and slid on the proverbial banana skin into the shallow end of the pond. As he pushed wet hair off his eyes, Joe watched Hunter pick up and shake the snarling animal.

"What the pop is wrong with you, you stupid dog!"

Otis hopped in front of him and subtlety tipped his head towards his mistress. Hunter faced Teomichi, holding the growling dog at arm's-length. "Lady, you gotta do something about this dog."

She gave no indication that she heard him.

Kyle whispered, "You got to say something like 'your highness' before she'll listen to you."

Hunter shook his head at such nonsense. "Alright! Your queenliness, your enormity..."

At this, *la patrona* looked up. "Having some difficulty, are you? 'My lady' will do. Yes?"

"My lady," said Hunter, "your racist dog is going out of its way to attack me."

"I see. Chantico, come."

Joe plopped himself on the edge of the pool, looking on with the rest. The Chihuahua came to her mistress with her head up. Eyes met, a staring duel between the two.

"Dang," said Hunter. "That's one stubborn dog." Long minutes passed. As they watched, tears of blood oozed from the corners of the dog's eyes and dripped onto the cement. "This won't end well," said Kyle.

Still, neither duelist looked away. Teomichi slowly lifted one eyebrow. That action finally caused Chantico to yelp and close her eyes. She slowly lay down, spasms contracting her body, and rolled on her back. More long moments, more yips of pain until her mistress gently patted her stomach and looked at Hunter. "A reset, no?"

She returned to her computer screen. Chantico sat quietly at her feet.

"Dang," said Hunter. "I feel bad, like I just wanted her to keep it on leash, not give it brain-damage."

Joe looked at Teomichi, now dressed for her date. Fancier sandals, long black hair on her shoulders and a raw cotton tunic that showed off her only piece of jewelry: a pendant of ancient design, an ear of corn with jade leaves and gold kernels and silk. "The bark cloth jacket, Chantico."

When the doorbell rang, Joe jumped up. "I'll get it." Opening the door, he stared.

TezCat stood before him, smiling. "How convenient."

Chapter twenty

Fear pushed Joe flat against the wall. TezCat walked grandly to the patio and came back, escorting the demure Teomichi. As he allowed her to go first through the front doorway, Joe's enemy said, "I'll tell your dad I saw you."

Joe went right for his throat...and was hurtled back toward the kitchen. His hands were screaming hot and Joe raced to plunge them into the pool.

"What just happened?!" said Hunter.

"Call Gil!" said Joe, plunging his hands in the pool water. "Call him! Tell him TezCat was here! He knows where I live!" Joe felt sick to his stomach, again. Thinking he was going to die, *again.*

"Hey, Comstock," shouted his brother. Then, in a normal volume, said, "TezCat as in Tezcatlipoca?"

Joe lifted his head above the level of the deck. "How'd you know that? You are such a freak...I mean. I'm sorry."

A hard-to-read look passed over Martin's face before he responded. "Teomichi said she was seeing someone she's known forever. I looked up the list of suspects, so to speak. Can't see why he'd pick on you."

"Yeah, right?"

"And you burned your hands how...?"

"Grabbing him around the neck. Martin, he said, 'I'll tell your dad I saw you'. I lost it! But he must know where he is, huh?"

"Or he doesn't know and he's messing with you".

Hunter came over. "The Commander says we're to call him when the lady returns."

"Need some ice there, Ratty?" said Kyle.

"That's it?" said Joe. "We just wait?"

Kyle handed him two bags of frozen corn. "That's it."

Hunter nodded. "We just wait."

From her lounger, Zima said, "I don't know vhat Michi see in that man. Iz more to man than hair in bun."

"And *she* has the personality of a cold tortilla. But fish is family, as they say. Is there a paper to read? Any news of this place?" asked Bunya.

"Um," said Joe, happy to hold ice bags instead of play waiter. "I have the *Enquirer*. It's in my room, I don't care if you go in. It's the room next to the kitchen," Joe said from the pool.

"Maybe tomorrow. Isn't there a single shiny magazine with the best boutiques and restaurants?" The redhead looked around at unhelpful faces. Sighing, she said to Kyle, "Mister, uh, big blond man. What is this zombie problem?"

"Well, ma'am—"

"I'm far too young to be a 'ma'am'".

Joe noticed Otis—helping himself to caviar—lift his feathered forehead in serious contradiction.

"Well," said Kyle. "People have been eating *something*—we don't know what—that makes some people die. And some of them come back as zombies."

"Ah," said Bunya. "Nosferatu."

"Almost," corrected Martin. "These zombies prefer brains to blood. And they are out day and night."

"I had husband like zat," said Zima. "He give me good villa."

The afternoon crawled on. Hunter went out for supplies. When he returned, he got Joe in a chair, switching out frozen carrots for corn. "People are starting to take this zombie thing seriously. Not a lot of people out, but those who are, are stocking up on water and toilet paper and stuff." He handed Bunya a copy of the *Santa Barbara Magazine* and the *Wall Street Journal* to Martin.

"You're a life saver," he said.

Hunter smiled. "I didn't know what her Queenliness reads..."

"The *Corn News*," said Martin.

"Right."

"No, really," said Martin. "She's all about the horticulture of corn. White corn. Tortilla corn. *Elote*."

"And this is for you, little warrior." Hunter cautiously knelt down beside Chantico. "Peace, okay?" He opened up a little package of Cheetos.

The dog sniffed and touched the tip of one orange bit with her tongue. A little maneuvering with her paw and she bit off a section.

"Woof!" The dog trembled with happiness. She nibbled and chomped; she licked and chewed. By the end, the Chihuahua's lips, claws and tongue were screaming bright orange.

"Gracias," she sighed, lying contentedly on her side.

"What time is it now?" said Joe. "Wonder what's going on in the crisis—". He caught Kyle's warning look.

"It's 4 o'clock and all's well," Kyle said.

Joe drifted off to sleep on his recliner and dreamed that Otis was shouting, "Incoming!"

He opened his eyes. Kyle and Otis were both shouting, "Incoming!"

"Otis," said Kyle, "gimme some Recon!"

"Everybody," shouted Hunter, "into the house."

Bunya flew past Joe and his frozen carrots, slamming a bedroom door above before Joe got to the library across from the kitchen. He sat by the window where he heard Otis report to Kyle. "A party of five is attempting to scale the rock cliff at the end of the garden, sir."

"You and the dog get inside."

"We're quite impervious to any organism if you need us, sir."

"Kyle." Hunter called him to Martin's chair.

"Leave me alone," said Martin.

"Right," said Kyle. "Lift up your arms, same carry."

"I don't want to go."

"Di-rec-tor's son," said Hunter. "You will *not* give me a reason to punch your lights out. Arms up, NOW." They quickly dumped him the library couch.

"Look!" Joe shouted. A hand with forearm and head was showing above the cliff.

"It's all about the reach, gentlemen!" Finn came in with two broadswords in his arms. "These babies are so long the zombies won't be able to reach you."

Joe caught the "you". Hunter and Kyle exchanged worried glances.

Only Zima remained outside. She lifted her arms from her lounge chair towards Hunter and said, in a tremulous voice, "Help?"

"She's messed up," said Hunter, going for the door latch. Kyle blocked him with his arm. "You're not going! She can get her own sorry can out of that chair."

"Gotta," said Hunter. "Besides, they're just crawling."

Otis spoke up. "Let us run defense, good squires. Chantico?" The two raced out the door, the bird dive-bombing, aiming for eyeballs, now that three reanimates had scaled the cliff. The dog sank her teeth into disintegrating Achilles tendons.

"All right," said Kyle, exasperated. He grabbed a sword. "Joe, man the door." With Kyle watching his back, Hunter grabbed Zima like a hundred pound of cement and dumped her on the couch next to Martin. The seamen stood at the door, studying the steady progress of the deadly zombies. "Now, what?" said Kyle.

"Maybe they pound their heads till the windows break, I don't know," said Hunter.

The tone of low voices registered in Joe: they were afraid! His fearless burly guys were scared. *I get it. They'll die. One scratch and they're gone.*

He saw them in Dario's place. Kyle fevered; Hunter strapped down. Both dying. Joe knew lopping the heads wouldn't be bloody; he was tall, had long enough arms. And the sword was five feet long. Just had to stay out of reach.

Time to make a diversion to get past the Rat Patrol...like what? Twenty feet before they get to the door. Think, Lab Rat, think!

"Where're you going?"

"Bathroom," Joe said. He still needed a distraction. He picked up a tumbler of ice water and threw it on Zima who yelled. Hunter turned, Kyle stepped towards her and Joe grabbed a sword.

"Oh, crap!" He could barely grip it with his burns.

"And where are you going?" said Hunter.

"Help me lift this thing, Hunter, or you guys are going to die. I can at least do some damage."

The men looked at him. "Are you sure, dude?"

"Yep. I can do this." He met their eyes."

"Five of them," said Hunter. "The last one can barely move so you have a little time."

Kyle glared. "You cannot mess this up." Hunter lifted the broadsword and wrapped Joe's burned palms around it as he hissed with pain. Kyle opened the door. "Do it!"

"For Dario," he whispered. "For Dario," he said. "For Dario," he shouted. "For Dariooo," he screamed.

Through a veil of red, Joe sliced the sword down through the neck of the nearest zombie. The sword reverberated on the cement and one hand slipped off. He gripped it again, feeling only rage.

Head number two, clean.

Head number three, two hits.

Head number four. Head number five!

He turned a full circle, looking, panting.

"I am King Rat, I am King Rat!" he hollered. "I am King Rat!!"

"Dang," said Hunter, now standing beside him. "It looks like Fright Night Bowling out here!"

"Or old-time rugby," said Kyle who pushed the tip of the other sword into the corpses, making for certain the heads were separated from their bodies.

"Okay, little buddy, let's get you inside," said Hunter. "You were mighty out there, Joe."

"I am King Rat!" Joe said, still gripping the sword handle for all he was worth.

"Deep breath, little buddy, let it go." Hunter held out his hand. "Let it go. Give it to me."

Joe slowly relinquished his weapon. He stared at his palms. "Whoa, my hands hurt."

Sitting again in the library, Finn opened the door for the Chihuahua. Chantico carried a long leaf of aloe vera, neatly cut by Otis's beak. "Thanks," said Joe. He looked for Otis and saw him in his usual post, on the security light.

"You notice?" said Kyle, "no tails." He, Hunter, Finn and Joe were sitting in the midst of the carnage, poolside, as it were. Zima had joined her sister upstairs and Martin had returned to his lair, using his arms, they assumed. He had said not a word.

Hunter spoke up. "You wonder, don't you? This nasty old batch—no tails. Maybe tails are like rigor mortis, they're there for the first few hours and then, nothing. Back to legs."

Finn, who had been smoothing aloe sap on Joe's palms, stood up straight. "What! Say that again?"

Hunter repeated himself. "I think that zombies only get tails for a few hours."

"Brilliant, brilliant!" Finn left them, hastening to his tech cave.

"I'm brilliant," said Hunter.

"Can I have a beer?"

"You're like what, fifteen?" said Kyle.

"Like sixteen in April! And I just wacked the heads off five people!"

"And your first response is beer." Kyle shook his head.

"You make that sound like a bad thing."

"It's disappointing, Joe."

He sighed. "Dad told us we were a family that couldn't drink," Joe paused. "Too easy to become alcoholics, he said. I didn't care after he disappeared and I had a buddy—"

"We get the picture. Personally," said Kyle, standing, "I want to thank you."

Joe shrugged, embarrassed. "Whatever."

Hunter stood up, furious. "What the pop do you mean, 'whatever'? You say 'you're welcome' to the man! And you stand like a man!"

Joe stood. He muttered as instructed and shook the hand Kyle extended, grimacing.

"You don't get to save lives every day. It's special." Hunter put out his hand. "Thank you, Joe Comstock."

Joe stood taller. "You're welcome."

Hunter laughed and gave him a hug. "Okay, have some of this."

Joe guzzled some Mexican coke, loving the cold glass bottle on his blisters. "Did Martin leave?"

Kyle went downstairs and returned. "Gone."

Chapter twenty one

They sat quietly looking on as Melusine's workers collected samples from the corpses. Behind them were the Santa Barbara police. "Sad-looking bunch," said the officer. "Yeah," said Finn, who had let them in. "A really slow bunch. But it gave me time to get the sword, you know." As Ratty and his guys listened, Finn took the glory for the multiple beheadings.

Hunter signaled for Joe to be cool. "He's in charge of Public Relations."

The seamen scrambled to stand and Joe—holding more frozen vegetables—turned to see Gil coming from the front. "Boopdiddly, I missed the party. Sit, gentlemen. *Finn* did the chopping?" They turned to see Finn pantomiming all his fancy swordplay.

"Yessir," said Kyle, as Hunter pointed toward Joe, hiding the pointing finger with his other hand.

"Fuzznuts!" Commander Muirgen nodded, and nodded some more. "Well done."

"Do I get a prize?"

"What do you want?"

"No more "Fuzznuts", sir. I don't care if it's military tradition. I don't like it."

Gil looked around the gore-strewn patio. "Five heads? Yeah, I think that counts. You are no longer Fuzznuts. Joe it is."

"Thank you...sir." He felt happy and ridiculous, sitting with hands in the air, holding frozen veggies, braced on his elbows.

"What have you learned, Joe?"

"You sound like my dad." Joe smiled sadly. "I learned that beers are hard to get, sir—and that's okay. And that protecting people is different than...I don't know. It's not like eating slugs or worms 'cause they dare you, but it's "I will never back down". I didn't know they were different...it's a way different thing."

"You're talking about the courage born of love, young man. Men, at attention." Commander Muirgen, Seamen Kaufman and Blount stood. "Joseph Comstock, we salute you."

Something burned Joe's eyes as they raised their hands and gave a smart focused salute. He could not speak.

"And," continued the Commander, "I'd love a cup of coffee."

When Joe came back with a hot mug-full—on a saucer so he didn't have to feel the heat—they were talking about his brother to Finn.

"Finn?"

"He's on the computer perhaps 16 hours a day when he's here."

"Who's he talking to?" said Gil. "Is he gaming?"

"I taught him how to build a computer from scratch. You know, 'a useful life skill'. He never seemed interested in gaming. He wanted access to libraries and political sites."

"He wanted to be governor," said Joe.

"I need to know where he's going on-line. Matter of security, Finn."

Finn looked uneasy. "I taught him well...hmm, I might be able to get a cookie through."

"Gentlemen, I need an accurate read on Martin. He's the Pacific Trues commander. Joe?"

"He's a mess. He was shouting at a girlfriend my mom sent him." He shook his head. "Like how gross is it to have your mother pick your girlfriend? He was trying to dump her 'cause she's a perv. And he really doesn't want to talk to me. Keeps telling me to leave, but he agreed to stay today...and now he's gone. Sir, can you get my brother a decent girlfriend?"

Hunter and Kyle looked at each other.

Gil answered. "That would take a very special candidate, Fuz—Joe. Look, we've received a flippergram off Peru. We need to follow up on some possible zombie orcas. Seamen, is Martin up to the job?"

"Sir," said Kyle, "all of Comstock's work has been good." Hunter nodded his agreement.

"Fine. We'll assume he's still at Peggy's Bar. Bannerman's pounding out details with the Peruvians. We'll reassess Martin just before the mission." He paused and studied Joe's blistered hands, now oozing from the sword. "Joe, Luz Marina will be here Saturday morning to draw blood. Make sure she sees these. The Rat Patrol stays with you here. And Cheyenne?"

"Upstairs with the fish, sir."

"God bless her. Well, Mellie's got her samples—no tails, right? Spinmaster Finn, you'll work your PR magic. Was that your masterpiece: "Ocean fish suspected of carrying zombie virus"?"

"It was approved at the highest levels."

"It's brilliant. Give the populations a chance to recover and...oh."

Joe looked up. Gil's eyes were fixed upon Teomichi who had just come in, alone.

She studied him and quietly asked, "Have we met?"

"No ma'am." Gil shook his head. "Pardon my rudeness, but you look very much like someone I knew."

"Someone you loved, perhaps?"

"Yes, ma'am. My wife."

"If you'll pardon *my* rudeness," she continued. "Was she Mexicana?"

"She was Siksika, Blackfoot. Perhaps we could speak another day."

Teomichi gave a small nod. "Otis will let you know my availability." She calmly scanned the zombie dead, and walked back into the house and up the steps, Chantico at her heels.

Kyle motioned with his chin where Otis perched. Gil shook his head. "Call me," he said quietly and left, hands in his pockets for the only time Joe could remember.

Joe decided on a shower in his humble maid's quarters—a super-quick cool shower with blistered hands. Sitting again in the library with his hands slathered with more aloe vera goo and propped above his heart, he and his bodyguards laughed at Key and Peele's "White Zombies".

Tomorrow's Friday, thought Joe, as sleep was coming on. Saturday I see Rachel. Saturday, I can leave the asylum.

When Joe got up the next morning, the back lawn and patio had been returned to their tidy Californian splendor. Teomichi was back on her laptop in her lawn chair, with Chantico at her heels. And Cheyenne was attending the fish ladies. Joe suspected Hunter or Kyle had begged her to stay.

"And I thought you might like this," the beautician said, handing the *National Enquirer* to Zima.

"Look, look!" Said Zima. "Is Vodnik! Listen: 'Fish man over ze Falls.' Is Vodyanoy."

"Do you know him?" said Joe.

"Of course, iz fish of long time."

"Not our favorite fish," added the redhead. "He is really quite disgusting. Somehow, he always manages to be slimy, even in Cannes."

"And bad clothz! No fish man should vear turtleneck!" said Zima. "Not with big neck. Bad look."

"I agree. He looks like a toad in a turtleneck." Bunya gave a moment's thought. "I don't think there is a good look for old Vodny."

Teomichi lowered her laptop. "This fish is a slime ball, as Americans say, whose singular goal is to irrevocably pollute Lake Baikal."

"But Michi," Zima said, aggrieved, "Fish is *family*."

"Here, let me read it." Bunya took back the paper and read. "Siberian Millionaire Survives Falls. Owner of Lake Baikal Paper and Chemicals Corporation, Vodnik Vodyanoy said going over Niagara has always been a top personal goal. "I love everything about Canada," he said. "Lake Superior, Lake Huron, Lake Erie, and my girlfriend. She's Canadian, too." Mr. Vodyanoy launched himself over the Canadian side of the Falls the next to the security camera— "I'm not going to do this twice", people heard him say—and came up below the rapids. The local magistrate is considering levying the maximum $10,000 fine. "I'd pay twice that much," said Mr. Vodyanoy."

"Lies," said Zima. "There no lives cheaper man. Bunya, we need speak to Niagara Indian girl."

"Why her?" said Bunya, raising an eyebrow. "When we can see Angeline. See the picture? I'm texting her, now." Bunya texted and waited.

"Ma'am, who exactly are you ladies?" asked Kyle.

"We are hydrophilic ladies," smiled the redhead.

"Ma'am, you have to translate that for me."

"We are Rusalka from Ukraine. Some people think we entrap men and drown them. What a crude notion. We think of ourselves as spreading our joy, fertility and beauty among the earth."

This time, it was *la patrona* who raised her eyebrows. She sat sipping espresso as Chantico, with hands again, was patting out fresh corn masa into flat rounds. Otis then cooked the tortillas on a portable comal. After they cooked on one side he would turn them with his beak. Cheyenne then put grated fresh Oaxaca cheese and salsa verde on them, and served them to Teomichi on Anne-Sirène's good china.

"Your turn, Joe", said Cheyenne, coming at him with the first aid box. Otis had snipped another blade of aloe vera which she slit and spread the gel on his palms and wrapped them with non-stick gauze and tape. Finn came outside with his cup of coffee. "Your brother's downstairs if you'd like to speak to him."

Joe descended the steps with dread. "Martin," said Joe.

Martin sat on the ledge of rock with his tail in the ocean. "Little brother, or King Rat, if you prefer. Slayer of zombies."

"And?"

"And I wanted it! I wanted the virus. But no, you and your 'posse' had to play hero." Joe realized no kudos were coming. "I swam out and looked for more, but Gling and Gil's Zombie Rangers have done too good a job."

"Tiresome," said Joe, using one of Martin's favorite words against him.

"Oh, the big hero now, using big words. Or the blabbermouth using big words."

"I can't be such a blabbermouth; they let me know about the mission tomorrow."

"Mission", said Martin. "What mission?"

Joe knew he had failed again. He looked at Martin who was smirking. "You knew, right?"

"Introducing Blabbermouth Joe, the weak link in a worldwide secret organization."

Joe was getting angry. "So my family makes a secret pact to let me think you were dead? Oh, I know what kind of family we are—"

"Wait for it, said Martin.

"We're a family for Martin, not for me."

"Presenting: Whiney Joe with his two good legs."

"Shut up, Martin. Could you stop being a jerk for one minute? For the last three months I've had nobody and—"

"I'm not a jerk, officially. Mother says I'm wallowing. So, I am officially a wallower. I am to make 'adjustments' .Well, here's an adjustment: when I die you can have my Dino Riders and my sneakers."

"What!? That's it? I want you to act like my brother and the best you can do is give me sneakers?!"

"And Dino Riders. They're originals!" Martin's great tail twitched side to side. "And I've outgrown the sneakers."

Joe could hardly breathe for rage. "Shut up! Shut UP! I just got you back and you want to give me some stupid lame toys! You're not dying. You're not leaving. And you will make whatever stupid adjustments you gotta make!" Joe looked up and saw Kyle looking in the doorway. He tried to catch his breath; he tried to cool down. "Least you could do..." More deep breaths. "...is give me something important."

"I bet your hands didn't hurt while you were yelling," said Martin.

"I hate you," he said, without passion.

"Maybe you should." The brothers sat in silence. Then Martin spoke. "I have a car, a panel truck, actually. It's in a vast old factory complex mom bought me in Duluth."

"Duluth?"

"Right on freezing Lake Superior. It's red brick with a high wall and plenty of parking. She said to use my imagination...maybe someday. You know Mother's rich, the empress of real estate? She's Oprah-rich."

"I guess," said Joe. "Like look at this place. I can't believe she shopped for us at Goodwill."

"What the rich will do for fun," said his brother.

"We could have taken more vacations."

"Always leave 'em whining," said Martin, as he slid into the water outbound, slapping water on his brother as he left.

Chapter twenty-two

It didn't matter the temperature, which was 62° by the thermometer in the kitchen window, the fish ladies sat by the pool every day, all day.

"There's one," said Finn, pointing to a drone in the sky. "That's a lot lower than 350 feet, I'm telling you. Are you going out today, kid?" Joe shrugged as he filled the coffee pot with water. "Grab a paper if you do. I want to see if they put in the rigor mortis and tail connection."

"You're in charge of merm PR, right?"

"Ah, the Best Right Light? Of course, what else?" He walked off, chuckling.

"Hunter's taking Cheyenne home." Kyle was loading breakfast pastries on a plate. "Nothing fancy today, I told them."

"Whoa, she was amazing," said Joe. "I didn't know anybody could have that much patience."

"Yeah...until she started talking about fish sticks."

They were serving when the doorbell rang. "My turn," said Joe, as much running away from the lazy fish ladies as towards the door.

"My Angeline," said the squat man before him with a booming voice. "She sick. Iz home Zima?"

Ah, the Enquirer photo dude.

"Iz Vodyanoy?" Her deep raspy voice sounded from the patio.

"Iz Zima? Bunya?" Now, Kyle was behind Joe, looming large. The fish man clicked his heels and gave a smart bow. "I am Vodyanoy."

"This is the fish dude who went over Niagara Falls," Joe said to Kyle. Kyle swept his arm to let him pass. "He does look like a toad in a turtleneck," Joe whispered.

"And *she* can actually walk," said Kyle, as Zima strode to meet him, giving a kiss on both cheeks.

"Voddy...Vhere is Angeline?" She peered over Vodyanoy's shoulder. "Boys," she smiled at Kyle and Joe, "you bring her in?"

"We're out of beds." As Kyle spoke, Joe noticed the damp footprints that trailed after "Voddy".

"She can have mine, "said Joe. "I'll take the couch in the library."

#

"This Angeline has all the signs, Gil...a few more hours, I guess. Could you bring those ratchet straps? No, I don't mind. Lab Rat duties."

Joe gave the pretty woman Tylenol and put cool washcloths on her head, which he had to keep centering on her forehead as she moved her head side to side. "Young master," said Otis, balancing on the bed post, "What can I do to be of assistance?"

Joe considered the question. "Tell them Kyle and Hunter cannot come into this room, for any reason. So, you or I will have to bring in whatever to the Fish. And pretty soon, when Gil comes, we'll be 'securing' her to the bed. Would you tell them they can come in now...thanks, Otis." The cormorant pointed to his wristwatch above the joint of one leg. Joe held out two, then three fingers and shrugged.

He ended up sitting outside the room. Best place to run interference for his Rat Patrol. Kyle scoured the house for three chairs small enough to fit in the room where Zima, Bunya and Vodyanoy waited with the now incoherent Angeline.

Otis hopped down the steps. "Mister Finn," he heard Otis say, "My lady requests the linens on the beds be laundered. It has been three nights."

Finn tramped up the steps like a condemned prisoner as Kyle and Hunter came through the door. "You found a newspaper?!" He grabbed it. "The bird says it's time to wash the sheets!" Finn said, as he hot-footed it back to his cave.

They were taking armloads of bedding to the laundry room when Gil came in. "We want extra pay, Commander."

"I'm sure there's a hazard there somewhere, men."

Gil helped Joe strap the dying mermaid down. Then, they sat outside the room. "My Eagle died of a fever. And then our boy. She died hard, but he just flew away with her."

"Aren't you afraid of this fever," Joe asked.

Gil shook his head. "I'm not afraid of dying, son. That old man in the station wagon? That's what I'm afraid of—when nobody needs the strength of my arm...or even my fine singing." Sounds of grief came from the room. Gil looked at his watch. "We'll need to get her out of here within the hour." He made a call. "Mellie, come now if you want samples. I'm shipping her out ASAP.

"Bird," said the commander to Otis. "Would you ask if your Lady would meet with us in the library? And Kyle, I'll need you and Hunter, too."

In the doorway of the sickroom, Zima stood and struck the tragic pose of an opera singer. "Ve make vake!"

"Vake?" said Kyle.

"Foods and vodka and talks of Angeline."

Oh, *wake*, thought Joe. "I'll send in Otis."

But Otis was attending his lady in the library. *La Patrona* of Lake Chapala sat in the overstuffed leather chair with Chantico at her feet as the men sat in a loose semi-circle around her. "You, too, Joe," said Gil. "This is mainly about you."

That set off trip wires of alarm. *Now what?*

"We thank you, great Lady, for this audience. I offer this poor gift." Gil presented a long jeweler's box, an old box. Inside was a bracelet of gold panels, each thick with a cabochon of rich jade. Joe could see it fit with her corn pendant necklace.

She nodded her acceptance. "Speak."

"You have come to the house of Joseph's mother"—*Yeah, lady, I'm not the pool boy*—"to vacation with a fellow Aztec deity."

She frowned. "I am Nahua. He is Aztec."

Gil accepted her correction. "He is what we police sorts call 'a person of interest'. I call him Mister Smoke and Mirrors."

She laughed. Miss Bland Tortilla Chip laughed! "I cannot tell you how exactly correct you are. That is what he is called in his own language."

Gil continued. "Everywhere he goes, fires erupt, explosions blast, revolutions start. I am not comfortable with him even being in this city. And every time he has seen this young man, he's threatened him with death. What is he up to? And, a most impertinent question, why are you with him?"

"The second question first. He is with me because I am *not* his Bat. My role is to create jealousy in her."

"His paramour. Who is she?"

"We do not name her." Chantico began to tremble. Teomichi touched her head, giving her fingers, and allowed the dog to fasten the bracelet upon her wrist. "I have agreed to go out with him because I do not wish him for an enemy. And I am stand-offish toward him because I want no want retribution from her."

"No other reasons, great Lady?" said Gil.

Joe was expecting lightning bolts to strike.

But she was indulgent. "They are good reasons, Commander. But I hope to be given a boon, as well. My cousin, Chalchi, "stepped out" with him the last cycle and he gave her a villa near Cancún."

"You have been so very generous, Lady. May I ask the boon you wish?"

"I shall ask for water rights along the Rio San Juan that feeds my lake. My ability to grow good crops is not under my control as I wish it to be. Now to your first question: what he is 'up to'... Otis, you shall answer."

"The great cycle of life is restarted every fifty-second year, Commander. It is the duty of He-whose-slaves-we-are to make the sun come up the morning after all the fires of the land and temples are extinguished."

"How?"

"I tell," said Chantico. "The high priest of the royal temple take heart from brave warrior and start new fire on his chest. New fire sent by running people to all places and Tezcatlipoca make rise the sun. Everybody make fiesta!"

"Except the warrior," said Kyle.

Gil indicated Joe. "Why him? He's not a warrior."

The bird looked him straight in the eye. "He was yesterday."

Gil was silent a moment. "I can go in his place."

The Lady gently shook her head at Gil. "You are—what is the expression—long in the tooth, Commander. The gods demand a courageous youth."

Warrior Joe was ready to throw up.

"Has he ever said Joe was his choice, Lady?"

"It has never come up in conversation."

Gil crossed his arms, now standing and pacing.

Teomichi continued. "I do not know if you can protect the boy, Commander. You should know that the new moon is this week. Sunset is at six-thirty, and Orion's belt can be seen above the horizon six hours later. That will be the time for the sacrifice."

"Twelve-thirty," Gil said to himself. "A theological question, finally, my lady. Would He-who-etc-etc play both the role of priest and god? In other words, would he *make* the sacrifice and *accept* the sacrifice?"

"Hmm. Somewhat like your Trinity." Teomichi studied the question. "For myself? I would not." She shook her head. "No, no I would not. What would the other gods say? But as for Tezcatlipoca, I don't think he would care, one way or the other."

She stood, concluding her audience. The men stood as she passed.

La Patrona paused. "Remember the new moon, Commander."

"Meaning?"

"It will be most dark."

Chapter twenty-three

"Bunya, look you for Russian deli? Goood. Ve vant cutlets and potato, sausage and borscht and blini...NOBODY THEY EAT LUNCH! Ve eat Siberian funeral!"

"Zima, I have standards, truly I do." Bunya stood, confronting her Rusalka cousin. "Therefore, I will not eat blini from a store. I will go with the men and buy all we need. I merely ask you to organize the kitchen so that I may fry the blini when I return. " She rolled her eyes at another of Zima's tragic postures and then looked at Gil. "It would be lovely were you to invite Luz Marina and Melusine. Zima would love to have a cast of thousands...as Michi may chose not grace us with her presence."

Bunya looked between Kyle and Hunter. Hunter tipped his head towards Kyle.

Joe happily piled into the back of the SUV. He took the iPad, played navigator, and soon they were parked in front of Yume's Russian Emporium. As Bunya filled a tiny kid-sized shopping cart and Kyle went next door for a dozen bottles of vodka, Joe took charge of nonalcoholic drinks. Sour cherry juice—four of those, as Zima had pressed him to find it, went into his cart. *Whoa*, "Samovar Sweetened Tea with Extra Lemon Pulp"! The product had the word "NEW" next to it in red lettering. *So okay*! Joe put two of those in his cart, a few bottles of apricot kompot, some sparkling water, and two six-packs of Mexican Coca-Cola...Joe imagined drinking Mexican Coke during a Siberian blizzard.

Checking out, the owner paused and switched to English, staring at Joe. He raised his eyebrows. "You like borscht? I tell you, this borscht is veery good. My wife makes the best borscht. You eat with sour cream? Good." Then, he and Bunya went back to speaking Russian. She pointed at a bag of chewing tobacco which he added to the pile.

Back at his mom's, they parked beside the USCG car. Walking inside, he heard Melusine say, "You could have let me know sooner. I could have at least brought you a body bag, Gil.|"

"Mellie, by this point, I've got my own supply."

Joe came in the house with his bags of beverages as Doc B's men took Angeline out in her body bag.

"Joe," Kyle called, "put the drinks in the bar outside."

"Okay. Hi, Luz Marina," he said. Joe figured they were here for the wake.

That outdoor refrigerator was below the library window. In rows, Joe placed the Coke, the kompot, sparkling water, sour cherry juice and, last, the NEW Samovar Iced Tea…and looked closely at the pulp in the bright March sunlight reflecting off the Pacific Ocean below.

The hair on his arms rose. *A virus in a bacterium…*

"Doc!" he shouted. "Come here! You gotta see this!"

Melusine, Gil and Luz Marina quickly surrounded him on the patio.

Joe poured a little in a glass tumbler and held it to the light. "Since when," he said, "does lemon pulp have eyes?"

Melusine grabbed the tumbler. "Oh, my," she breathed.

"It's the source, isn't it? Krill's a crustacean like shrimp!"

"You okay, Joe?" said Hunter from the kitchen.

"He's just being brilliant," said Melusine, still staring through the glass and shaking her head. She passed the glass and each of them saw an occasional strand of pulp that had the tiniest black dot at one end.

"A virus in a bacterium in a krill," breathed Luz Marina. She grabbed the bottle and read aloud, "Made in cooperation with Lake Baikal Beverage Corporation." She looked horrified at Gil.

"Time to talk to a fish," he said.

But Bunya stood blocking the French door back into the house. She held out the bag of tobacco. "Give him this. He tends towards bad behavior."

"Give him a *gift*?" said Melusine. "I want to gut him!"

Bunya rushed ahead and dropped the tobacco on his lap. "But I will be sick, Vodyanoy, if you swill that into a can. Smoke it or swallow it," said Bunya and tucked next to Zima who was holding his hand.

The grieving fish man looked right and looked left at Gil and Melusine and Luz Marina. The rest crowded around the doorframe of the maid's room. He stuck a wad of tobacco in his wide, drooping jaw. He chewed it very slowly and finally swallowed it with effort. "Vhat? Vhy you angry peoples at vake?"

Gil held up the bottle of iced tea. "Tell me what you know."

He made a long face. "My people find giant, ancient, Siberian bacterias and wiruses. I tell Aztec. He like this. One night, we drinking wodka in Baikal. I tell him that mermaid ladies never go parties with me, never wisit, never return email. I hate mermaid ladies, I tell him. This vas before I go BaitDate.com and meet my Angeline."

"And?"

"And he say that merm ladies vill feel bad for not being nice to me."

Melusine pointed to the empty bed. "Well, that one feels bad for sure.

Luz Marina held up the bottle. "Did she drink this? Did you?"

"Both. We like. It make her sick?"

Melusine nodded.

"I cannot stay here," said Luz Marina. "I will take it and confirm." She looked at Vodyanoy with undisguised revulsion.

"Vas Aztec," Vodnik Vodyanoy moaned. "Aztec make Vodyanoy cry. But I take it like fish. Wery brave fish. But vhy she die and I not die?"

"Because you are a miserable, sodden fish," said Melusine.

"*This* is vhy I complain to Aztec," said Vodyanoy to Gil. "Mermaids no nice."

"Shut up," said Gil.

"No, I no shut up. I tell you von more thing because Aztec lie. There is other i-ced tea. Name kootly something."

"Got it, ma'am," said Kyle, holding up his smart phone. "Cuāuhtli Sweet Tea with Lime Pulp."

"I'm coming with you," said Melusine.

"First," said Luz Marina, "I must *saludar* to Lady Michi."

"No go! Ez funeral," cried Zima. "Stay to eat!"

The sun had set a while ago. Finn and the fishes had already gone through a mountain of food and six bottles of vodka. Gil told Vodyanoy that he and the Rusalka would both be gone in the morning and confined the wake to the dining room. He, the burly guys, and Joe were watching CNN in the library.

"There it is," said Kyle.

"See if it's on the other channels," said Finn. They were looking for the special alert he had engineered to stop the sale and consumption of both brands of iced tea.

"It's viral!" Finn grinned. "My very best work. Twitter, Facebook, Instagram, Youtube. Tiktok. Everywhere! Everywhere in English and Spanish."

"We're done, then." Gil sat with his Coke. "It's off the market. Luz is working on a vaccine. We've done what we can do."

"We don't go back to the ship until Rachel's game, do we?" said Joe. He looked down. Chantico was leaning against his legs, gently swaying.

"The door, please, *por favor*."

"Are you drunk?" Joe asked. A belch that should have come from the belly of a St. Bernard was his answer. "Don't fall in," he called after her as she pin-balled her way to a tree.

"Hold that door, young master. I am in no condition to fly." Hunter shook his head watching Otis stagger on webbed feet out the back door. "But food was good…"

Nobody said anything to that. "What's next, Commander?"

"Retracing distribution routes. Red's on that. Setting up local centers where people can drop off what they have left. It's up to the Centers for Disease Control after that."

"And, if people keep any, it's like having a loaded gun."

"It's a biological weapon. Joe, you have far too thorough an imagination."

The front door rang and they heard Chantico bark furiously. "The *front* door?" said Hunter, as he pushed himself out of deep leather chair. Joe went with him, tired of sitting. Hunter opened the door and went flying backwards.

Joe stared. There, in hip hop gear, stood the son of the king of the heavens himself! With a flick of his royal wrist, Joe was moving into the back seat of a waiting SUV. He had no ability to resist.

"In!" Tezcat ordered Chantico, and the dog jumped up next to Joe.

As the car door slammed, Joe heard Gil shouting his name, and, as he watched, the front door burst into flames.

Chapter twenty-four

"That's my trademark. 'Tezcatlipoca, firebrand'…and liar and creep?! Is that what you're thinking?"

It was. Joe blocked his mind with "Dom the Dad" over and over, the best mantra he could come up with.

"Knock it off. Pretend you don't know I can read minds. It's not as fun when I tell people. And, yes, we're going up the hill. Oops, there I go again."

Joe felt Chantico next to him, trembling. The car went through the streets and up, winding towards the base of the mountains. *Queen* was blasting through the sound system. *It's the terror of knowing what the world is about*
Watching some good friends screaming

"Tonight's entertainment will be brought to us by *Queen*—the best music of the twentieth century. And our playlist will include <u>Under Pressure</u>, <u>We Will Rock You</u>, and last and *certainly* last, <u>Another One Bites the Dust</u>."

"Do you know where my dad is?"

"No."

"Should I believe you?"

"Absolutely not!" Tezcatlipoca floored the gas pedal and almost instantly slammed on the brakes. He opened the car door and turned to them in the back seat. "Let me go have a look around. If he moves, rat dog, rip his nose off."

Chantico whispered. "Por favor, do not move."

"You'd rip my nose off?!"

"He-whose-slaves—"

"Yeah," said Joe. "Got it."

"He told me I did not have to fast."

"Ooh, back in the day," said Joe. "And you believed him."

"He is son of the sky king—oh, they are talking of you!"

"Who? Where?"

"Great lady and the fishes. They tell my Lady to make He-whose-slaves-we-are jealous."

"You can hear it?"

Chantico nodded.

"And that's it?!" said Joe. "That's the whole strategy to save my life...?" He sunk his head into his blistered bandaged hands. "And another one bites the dust."

Tez opened the car door. "This will do very nicely. Out! You too, *esquincle*."

They were standing in front of a transformer station, the deep threatening electrical *MMMMM* pulsing through their muscles, aggravating their nerves.

Joe could not make his feet move. "Are we talking human sacrifice, then?"

"I'd say so, yes. I don't go through the trouble every time. I never have trouble getting dead warriors every 52 years. Your United States of America is a dependable source of wars, or the Middle East or Asia. Wherever."

"Why me," asked Joe.

"Let's see. Ebola didn't really take off. And I like to see progress. Yes, I'm a man— a *supaNAtural* man—who likes to see progress. The zombie virus had real potential and then *you* had to come along and be immune."

"Aren't you too late? They already have my blood; they are making a vaccine."

"Exactly."

"Why not cut the heart out of a zombie?"

"Wait, wait. I like this song" He gave a little bit of hip hop arm dazzle and sang along. *You got blood on yo' face, You big disgrace*

Wavin' your banner all over the place.

We will, we will Rock you...

He pointed at Joe. "You might have been a zombie. BUT, you lucky boy, you get to be part of something historic, a genuine old-school event!" He looked at his watch. "It's 12:25 and Orion's belt will show up around 12:30 and then it's...Show Time! 'Please enjoy the music while you wait.'"

"Will it hurt?" said Joe.

"I hope so." The Aztec deity added some hip-hop slides and spins on the sidewalk, crooning, "I'm supaNAtural, I'm supaNAtural."

I have nothing to lose, thought Joe. "Yeah, they'll let anybody in."

Tez stopped dancing and frowned. "My brother says that."

Direct hit. Don't fail me now, Wikipedia. "Quetzalcoatl?"

"How do you know?"

"I know stuff," said Joe. "This sacrifice will actually feed *him*, won't it?"

"You're stupid. You're wrong!"

"And you have to do the loser thing of being your own priest. Even Teomichi—a fish!—said she wouldn't stoop to that. She said the other gods would laugh."

"You see this?" His face furious, Tez held up a lighter. "I am going to start a fire on your chest after I take your heart out!" He looked at his watch. "In. Four. More. Minutes."

"Master," said Chantico. She pointed up with her muzzle. They all watched Otis slowly descend curbside, a tiny black rectangle in his beak. It enlarged to a glistening sports car. Then, a bag of jaguar-print fabric slid off his wings. "My Great Lady of Obsidian requests an audience, my Lord."

"The Bat, the Bat is here! Quickly, she can help, she can watch!"

Otis unzipped the case and a tiny bat stepped out. Otis gently placed her on the sidewalk. She emerged from the soles up. First, black, thigh-high suede boots blended into a jaguar pelt micro dress. Covering her shoulders and arms was a suede black capelet, with ribs stitched where bat "fingers" should be and dangling eagle claws hung at the ends. Her fingernails were very long and very black, her lips were screaming red and her hairdo was impossibly high.

"Bat, my adorable bat. You came to help!" She stood staring at him. "Say something, Bat. We have three minutes."

The Bat did not smile. "I just got a text from a little fishy. Are you really thinking of replacing me with that ear of corn, that bowl of grits?"

"Can't we talk about this later, my adorable one, my only? It's time for the sacrifice."

She stepped into his face and held up her finger. "Miss Tortilla Chip says you're celebrating with her tonight...Ah, you don't deny it!"

"But the sacrifice." Tez was definitely whining.

"You're pathetic. We don't count, *idiota*. The last genuine New Fire ceremony was 1507; somehow the sun has come up every morning since!" Her hands went to her hips. "I'm here, I'm now. You choose: you can take this kid's heart out and see if you can start a new fire rubbing sticks together like some deranged Boy Scout—"

"I brought a lighter!" He showed her, smiling.

"You are *totally* pathetic." She shook her head and rolled her eyes. "I'm not sure I want to be seen with you ever again."

"My bat, my bat! You can't be serious."

"You used to act like the son of the King of the Heavens, now you're just a second-rate, pyromaniac gangsta punk."

"What am I supposed to do?"

"Something better than this. Be a financier. That's destructive." She looked at her Apple watch. "You have ten seconds."

"Fine," Tez yelled. "But I'm going to have some fireworks." He grabbed Chantico and threw her into the transformer wires. Against the black sky, the fireworks of the system shorting out blazed high in a ragged circle. The lights of the communities went dark.

"My car," said the Bat, opening the driver's door.

"What are we driving?"

"A Jaguar, of course." The powerful engine revved and they drove off into the night.

In the blackness, the smell of Chantico's charred flesh carried on the air. Joe startled at a presence on his shoulder. It was Otis.

"Young master, you need to walk down this hill, starting this instant. Turn right at the bottom of the hill. You shall be walking west." Sirens were sounding and not that far away. "The commander should be able to find you easily."

"But what about Chantico?"

"I shall find her."

The bird bated. Joe watched his turquoise eyes glow like searchlights among the dangling black wires. Joe turned and walked swiftly down the hill. Within blocks, he was sitting next to Gil in the car.

"Where is he? Did he hurt you?"

"No. His girlfriend drove him off in a Jaguar." Joe sighed deeply. "I think Chantico is dead. He threw her onto the transformer."

Chapter twenty-five

All home, they waited for Otis in the pre-dawn stillness. Joe watched Gil stand behind Teomichi, his soldier's face etched with melancholy; she sat very still, slowly dragging the jade bracelet around her wrist.

Joe saw Otis first, and opened the back French door. The stench of burnt mammal filled his nostrils. The bird waddled through, a small charred lump in his beak.

Teomichi walked to the kitchen island counter. "Place her here, Otis." Her face was calm as she directed Gil's gaze to the cabinets behind her. "Commander, please place here this bowl and that bottle. Otis, I need my bag of elote." Her commands met, she mixed a paste of fine white corn meal with mescal and spread it on the charred half of Chantico, covering her disturbing burns.

Hunter watched intently, leaning in at the little dog's moans.

"Seaman Blount, Chantico would benefit from being held."

"She'll live?"

The immortal smiled softly. "It would be difficult for her to die. But I would like to her heal to be the best servant she can be."

"That's cold, Lady."

She handed him a kitchen towel. "We each have our place, Seaman Blount."

Hunter moved the Chihuahua as gently as he could onto the towel and sat with her against his chest. Joe heard him whisper, "Come on, baby girl", as Teomichi washed her hands.

Her announcement, "I am to my bed", was drown in a chorus of "Look! Look! It's them!"

On the television screen was a feed from a swimming pool down the coast, part of an Art Deco hotel. "Early this morning, CCTV cameras caught two alleged Aztec gods jumping off the heights of the Sunset Hotel in Hollywood. If you have any information, please contact..."

The six of them, plus Otis, stared at Tezcatlipoca and his Bat carousing in full regalia: feathers and beads and jaguar skins; metal strips and circles, lizard heads and eagles' beaks hanging from sashes. Skulls and arrows, bags and bundles, and mirrors of obsidian. Their bodies were striped with white, yellow, black, and red paint.

"Boopdiddly! That's about 14 stories high."

"Into eight feet of water...and they rocket back up!"

"Is that a knife?" said Joe. "I think she just cut his foot off!"

"That explains the limp," said Kyle.

"She is famous for her obsidian blade." Teomichi said. "The Aztec are always excessive. And he is without dignity."

"They look like they're straight off the pages of some Aztec book," said Kyle. The Codex Ixtlilxochitl," said the Nahua. She paused on the first step upstairs. "I owe Zima a great debt. She knows how to get rid of unsuitable men."

Gil nodded. "It's zero six hundred hours, men. Joe, the maid's room was cleaned by Mellie's staff. Your choice. Seamen, man the couches."

"Roger, sir."

#

"And he's finally up. Sluggy the Rat Boy."

Joe grinned. "Got a busy day!" He turned to Hunter on the couch. "How's Chantico?'

"Rff," she answered.

"Baby girl's coming around," said Hunter. He lowered his head as she whispered to him. "You sure?" The dog gave a small bark, so Hunter lowered her gingerly to the floor.

Chantico stood, then hobbled, then wiggled her hind quarters. "Ohh, I am well! Where is my lady?"

"Being waited on by Otis."

"She is great, my lady." As she spoke, Teomichi descended the steps with Otis behind her, carrying a tray. When she sat, she touched her calf and the dog went and sat by her. "I thank you, my Lady."

Teomichi spoke. "As I wait for my boon, I should like to give one to you, faithful helper. After a millennium in service, you might wish a respite. Hmm?"

Chantico looked at her mistress, eyebrows tilted. "I have never thought to serve anyone but you, Lady."

"You have been ill treated by He-whose-slaves-we-are and it grieved me to think you might have 'entered the water' from his cruelty. Seaman Blount, you may approach us. Will you accept the service of Chantico and care for her dutifully if I lend her to you as a pet?"

Hunter stood up. "I live on a ship, Lady. We don't have pets."

Gil spoke up. "Would you be willing to try?"

"What if Chantico doesn't like it?" said Hunter.

"She may call Otis," answered the demi-god.

Hunter picked up the Chihuahua and put her on the counter, eye to eye. "You can't be bitin' people because they ignore you, or you don't like them. Understand me, baby girl? Pets gotta let little kids dress 'em in baby clothes and drag 'em down the street on leases." He let that sink in. "And I might get married someday and she'd be your new boss, not me." Hunter leaned in, shaking his head. "And there will be no bleedin' eyeballs!"

The dog chewed on her lip. "Do I get more Cheetos? Can I bark at bad people and chase thieves?"

"Cheetos, yes. Thieves, yes. But I decide who the "bad people" are. And you need a new name to be my pet."

Chantico lowered herself onto the countertop and put her muzzle between her paws. She shifted her eyes between her lady and Hunter. Moments passed. "I like name Shakira." Her little dog face beamed while Otis rolled his eyes.

"I like Spike," said Hunter.

Teomichi gave a soft musical laugh.

"What it mean—Spike?"

Her mistress answered. "A big nail. And a big action."

The little dog showed all her teeth in a big grin. "I like!"

Hunter looked at Teomichi. "We done?"

"Almost. I am very fond of...Spike. I will be most displeased if you neglect her." She turned her eyes upon the dog. "I give you this boon of respite and the life of a pampered pet. When you return to me, you return as my slave. Do not forget."

Spike performed a beautiful downward-dog bow. "To serve you, Great Lady, is the highest pleasure." Teomichi waved her away and walked out to the patio.

"Sir," said Hunter Blount, gentling setting his new pet on the floor. "Permission to get more bandages for Ratty."

"Go on," said Gil. "The two of you."

Hunter looked at Kyle. "It's now 11:23. Make sure he's sweet-smellin' when we get back." Kyle saluted.

Hunter turned to his new pet dog. "Come on, Spike, let's go.".

CNN was following three major stories: Aztec Weirdness in Santa Barbara, Fish Head Fever Source Discovered, and an earthquake in Central Asia. Gil turned off the sound and poured yet another cup of coffee. "Bird, answer me this" he said. "Does she love that dog?"

Otis answered, "That is perhaps an overstatement the matter, Commander. My lady Michi loves *elote*, her white corn. My lady has *compassion* for Chantico."

Finn emerged from his lair. "What's that tapping?"

Joe looked and saw a substantial black bird tapping at the French door window. "Otis," called Joe. "You got company!"

Otis waddled to the back door. "Master Joseph, if you please?"

He opened the door and the two birds conversed in Avian. Finally, the envoy extracted a small manila envelope from a messenger bag with his beak. Otis accepted it with a bow, offering him water from Chantico's bowl. The raven declined. After much bowing and chirping, the bird turned, hopped over the threshold plate and flew over the pool toward the ocean.

Otis hopped to the pool, laid the envelop at her feet, and did his enlarging trick. "For you, my Lady."

"My boon? Let us see." Teomichi drew out a bundle of papers. She smiled.

"He-whose-slaves-we-are has been generous. Otis, prepare to leave."

"Do we await the return of Spike?"

She shook her head. "Let her begin her new life. Commander, the actions of your seaman are your responsibility."

"I have no worries, my Lady."

#

The Fish and Rusalka gone, Gil, Kyle and Joe sat in the sun. "Why the long face, Joe?"

"Sir? TezCat is a terrorist, right?"

"No. No, he's not a terrorist. There is nothing political or revolutionary about his actions. He's a criminal. Technically, he's an outlaw or a psychopath. He believes that he lives outside the law, outside human morality—"

"So he killed Dario for *nothing*?" said Joe.

"He killed Dario and everyone else out of boredom. That's a powerful force, son. Kierkegaard says it's the root of all evil." Gil took a deep breath. "I'm not as old as that monster, but I know where boredom could lead me. So I put myself under authority, the authority of the Trinity, and that of the military. Far too many folks think they are free when all they are is alone and unguided...and most of them don't live to ninety, much less since pre-history."

The commander pulled out a comb and tamed his power cut. *He was leaving?* Joe wanted to keep the solid, sane Gil close for safety. "Where are you going?"

"To church...and you're going to a volleyball match. Gentlemen," Gil said, "get Joe to Westmont College for that game...oh, and Luz Marina's coming to get your blood pretty soon."

"Okay."

Joe put together what he hoped was an outfit that would scream KEEP ME at Rachel, and headed to the shower. He washed his hair, shaved, and then soaped up. His hand froze under his right armpit. What he'd assumed was a pulled muscle or, somehow, a more manly muscle, was now a fold of skin. Joe grabbed the shaving mirror from the hook and stared. He slumped his weight on the wall of the shower. He ran his fingertips along the inner flap which was about two inches long and felt tiny little slits of flesh, like human radiator fins.

Joe slid down the shower wall as the water coursed, unnoticed, over this body.

I'm going to end up like Martin...

Coming 2021

An Excerpt from Book two in the *Comstock Tails Series*—
Mermaids of the Necropolis

"...Happy Biiirthday, dear Lab Rat. Happy birthday to you!!!"

Joe stopped in mid-step, surprised by a two-layer cake blazing on the kitchen counter. He had just come from wrestling practice and now was surrounded by his new "swimmer" family. "Thanks, guys...it's not until tomorrow."

"And what sort of a surprise would that be, then?" said Finn.

"Fair enough." Joe looked around. "Where's Hunter?"

Kyle shook his head, his auburn hair freshly shorn. "Waiting on the Empress of Cheetos—Spike's working on a pot gut. My man Hunter did not know what he was getting into."

"No good deed goes unpunished," said Gil, leaning on the counter. "You going to blow out the candles, son, or are we going to pick wax out of our teeth?"

Joe sucked in air, stared at the sixteen flames, and blew them out with energy. He knew what he wished for. It had been three weeks and the gills were no bigger.

"You can sign on next year," said Captain Bannerman. "It'll be the best four years of your life."

"He'll need that year," said Gil. "He's behind a year in school."

Joe went after the cake knife on the counter, but Finn beat him to it. "I'm not worried," said Joe. "Otis said I could make great money being a butler. Six figures!"

"A man-servant?" said Finn, thinking as he pulled out candles from the icing. "That would be a fine calling if people weren't involved." He neatly cut the cake and put the slices on fine china. "To the patio, I think, in honor of a sunny April fool and his birthday."

Sitting in full sun, the captain sipped his coffee, swallowing with deep satisfaction. "Finn, you're a good man. Speaking of the joys of *terra firma*, Joe Comstock, we could play a game on that fine slate table down the stairs."

Joe gave a noncommittal shrug.

The captain looked at Gil. "I'm getting no respect here, Commander."

Joe shook his head. "It's just that I'm keeping my head in my books while I'm waiting for wrestling camp in July."

"That's July. This is April."

And hoping to see Rachel...without my hands all wrapped in bandages. On the Bad Day, three weeks ago, he had stood before her, basically dragged to the volleyball game by Kyle and Hunter. Of course, he didn't know what to do with his burned blistered hands swathed in gauze and, of course, she thought it was hilarious. "What do we have here, guys, a widdle wabbit?"

Gil had then helped him matriculate at the Catholic high school and told him to live his life. He was not Martin, Gil had said, and waiting to be defeated was no life at all. Joe now put all his energy into getting caught up.

Joe realized he missed a beat when the captain said, "Well, that's for the best as there's a small detail we'll be going on."

Finn looked at him. "And what would that be?"

"Oh, a bit of orca hunting. There's concern about possibly sick members of a pod off the coast of Peru."

"Do tell," said Gil, lifting an eyebrow in his lawn chair. "Would this be near Paracas?" Joe watched Finn look instantly alerted, too.

"Exactly," said the captain.

Into the secretive silence, Joe asked, "How do you hunt zombie orcas?"

"Carefully," said Gil.

"Very carefully," said the captain.

I wish to thank the following people:

Sam Wilson, for making Joe a better person.

Ruth Hartling, for clarifying cell biology.

Sofía García Hernández, for explaining CRSPR and knowing about elegant worms.

Leo Awodey, for editing skateboard technique and lingo.

Frank E Cunniff, cover art. Good stuff, huh?

Arkadij Schell through Vecteezy.com for Chihuahua photograph

Alejandro Pinzón, for appropriate Spanish vocabulary.

Andrea McNeill, youth librarian, for her glowing encouragement.

And Francis Pionati, my love, for being the marvel that he is.

About the Author

I never thought I was writing sci-fi fantasy. Everyone just seems so real--how much does if matter if they're totems anyway?

I am a nurse, a proud mom, a lover of science and neanderthals and fat bumblebees. I also wish my mother had let me take tap dancing...

You can contact me at fishheadfever@gmail.com. I'd love to know who is your favorite character!

If enough of you are interested, I may put up a website with photos of Otis and Chantico/Spike.

Barbara